I0686083

NO MATTER
THE SEASON

Kenneth G. Kruschka

Copyright © 2023 Kenneth G. Kruschka

All rights reserved

The characters and events portrayed in this book are fictitious. Any similarity to real persons, living or dead, is coincidental and not intended by the author.

No part of this book may be reproduced, or stored in a retrieval system, or transmitted in any form or by any means, electronic, mechanical, photocopying, recording, or otherwise, without express written permission of the publisher.

ISBN-13: 9798218331597

Cover design by: Ken Kruschka

Library of Congress Control Number:

Printed in the United States of America

CONTENTS

MOTOYA
AND REY

a shark and whale story

CHAPTER 1

I t was 26 years ago, to the day, that Motoya came into the "safe room," which was to be used as a place for her to hide and exist. Motoya was a 66-year-old female shark, and she was blind, so her biggest fallacy was being out of the water. Now, by deduction, it's not difficult to have figured out that she didn't stray too far from areas she'd known (to some degree anyway), back when she still had had her vision. The room is just a short distance from where the Southern Ocean meets an embankment at the property yards' shoreline, although there's an open 15ft area where the yard is flush with the Ocean; for easing a boat (or whatever) into the water. Don't get me wrong, the rest of the yard's slope towards the waterfront is a little steep, much like a small hill or flight of stairs' angle would be. Laying on a table in the "safe room" is an old issue of National Geographic magazine, which contains an article that highlights the sharks moving from the water to indoors. If you read the article, it mentions that: "...a group of at least 3 sympathizers were involved in escorting (moving) of the shark...uphill from the Southern Ocean's shore bank." There's only 1 picture in the magazine article, showing a woman with an outdated hairstyle (makes the timing of the photo seem even older) guiding Motoya out of the water. The article also mentions how they had moved the shark in broad daylight, though the move was supposed to be done at night for secretive purposes--the piece didn't state why, regarding the secret. For what it's worth, the 3 sympathizers mentioned in the article lived out their days answering questions about the shark with answers like: "He thought that I'd thought, that she 'd thought that I...," which is a tough post hoc justification for the relationship. Anyway, even the quietest secrets have a way of coming out...eventually.

Motoya's best friend in the Ocean was a

106-year-old female Orca whale, named Rey. Rey never liked when people referred to her breed as a "killer whale," like she'd heard people yell at her on recreational whale watching ships. Rey, having been around for a while, once heard a radio station tagged as "Songs by the Seashore," playing one titled "Lean on Me" and Rey thought it sounded beautiful--she started humming the tune to calm herself down, if she was frustrated. Rey, being patient and understanding (unlike other whales or sharks she or Motoya knew) offered to guide Motoya around, helping her find food and resting places, after witnessing first-hand the reprehensible act that caused the shark to go blind; Russia launched an air-based military attack on Norway, hitting over the water area Motoya was swimming in, when she was only in her early 20's. Try as she may, all Rey learned about what'd occurred back then, when she was just getting into her late 60's, was land people kept repeating the words "September" and "Cold response." Motoya was very grateful for having a friend in Rey, telling her "I love you" often...Rey was just as grateful for having Motoya as a friend, loving her like the daughter she'd never had but always wanted. Motoya knew deep down that without Rey she wouldn't have made it. For 40 years after the day when the sky seemingly fell into the Atlantic in anger, Rey and Motoya marched on as a team, swimming along merrily and enjoying each other's companionship to the fullest, but another tragedy was about to occur and change all that.

CHAPTER 2

On an average summer's night, Rey guided Motoya deeper into an area where the body of water quickly started getting shallow, noticing there was a tidal shoal sandbar between the Ocean's water from their side and unknown waters, just over the other side of the shoal. The area of seafloor near the shoal was rocky and vegetative, but the fish they'd come to eat were getting smaller and smaller, the shallower the water became. Rey enjoyed watching Motoya getting some joy out of the trip anyway. Motoya said to Rey: "Listen! Did you hear something like an airboat motor? ... I've heard one, years ago, and their propeller sounds very different from one that's submerged or even a paddle boats' does. Rey replied: "Yes, but it's not here, yet I thought I'd felt its reverb through the water, as if it was!" This didn't make any sense and the pair almost got out of the area as if they'd seen a ghost, but just then a 32' Hovercraft boat plopped in the water over the shoal's top, landing in the right above them and cruising onward like it was nothing. Rey and Motoya both heard someone from on the craft yelling "No beach out of reach." They both realized, at that moment, that the water reconnects...somehow...and that it must be deep enough to sustain fish if boats that size are on it--they both felt if a boat can do it, so could they--so being the superior species of the water compared to a fake species (a boat) they believed that if they'd use the current to their advantage, getting enough push force, hopping over the shoal was possible. By nighttime, high tide had come in and the two were able to cross over the shoal, just about as easily as the Hovercraft had done earlier. The two were surprised that the water on the new side of the shoal was much deeper than the side they'd come from but realizing that fact led to bringing on more realizations; one into another, into another. It was such an overpowering moment of thought that anyone (animal or human) experiencing something like it could only react by blinking and breathing--everything you'd thought you knew, getting tossed for a loop. It was a very Christopher Colombus discovering "new" land kind of moment for them.

The new waterside had all sorts of piers and docks and a marina, there were even Lagoon warning signs that were everywhere on buoys. There was one area netted off that was a little surprising, because the fish inside it had no way to come out till someone opened it--the repeating words stenciled in red spray-paint on the netting all said, "Fish Hatchery." Rey wondered if this area was a benefit or if she was risking her and Motoya's health being there, but then Motoya caught herself a nice sized muskie, just over by a pier landing and Rey was able to catch herself 2 in 1 quick maneuver too. There were campfires burning somewhere over on the dry land as well as wildflowers along the shoreline, so the whale and shark went up to the water top to smell them and appreciate them; they liked smelling new things together. They were also able to take in the sounds of frogs croaking on Lilypad and crickets chirping all around and the softness of the clean bottom of the area they'd discovered; no old tires or barrels or sunken toxic...God knows what's.

CHAPTER 3

Historically, from piecing together outside source's explanations, the technical aspects of what occurred next (best guessing anyway) are as follows: About 2 A.M. at a nearby barrier island water channel, a good distance from where Rey and Motoya landed over the shoal, a 77-year-old woman was at her property's shoreline, deciding about walking in the water to fill a pail she'd brought with her. There was a group of alligators who lived in the lagoon, and they saw the old woman coming, they also knew she was an old pro when it came to bucket filling and alligator killing; she always carried a Cold War era Kalashnikov .47 caliber, strapped over her shoulder, and she loved to introduce it to the gators when they came too close. The alligator in charge was named Chief Gator, who proclaimed to the others "Don't mess with her!" just the same time that Motoya and Rey came approaching upon the alligator's section of water. The gators all listened to their Chief about leaving the old woman alone, so they merely floated up to the water surface; allowing Motoya and Rey to casually swim past underneath them all while they were on their way to cross back over the shoal. Both the shark and whale had had a successful time in catching and eating some nice fish, so much so that they were about in a food induced coma (stuffed and relaxed, like after a Thanksgiving meal) anyway, so they didn't even notice the gators' presence. In the alligators' defense, they really were on their best behavior! Well, the old woman just happened to be waist-deep in the water when the gators, all at once, took to the surface--the entire congregation of them, as chance would have it, surrounding her. She was so startled by seeing all the gators' eyes glowing in the moonlight's reflection, she had herself a heart attack and died right there in the water. The gator's thought they'd be blamed for the women's death, and they feared that the humans would retaliate by hunting and killing every gator. As a logical fix, Chief Gator came up with a plan to move the old woman's body out to deeper water, trying to make it appear like she'd drown while taking a swim...plus, it would be daylight soon...he couldn't come up with a better plan--especially, when not wanting to cause a scene. A group of 2 of the strongest alligators were chosen to alternate in the job of dragging the body out into deeper water; if they got caught, they'd take the blame, alone, for the whole colony; sacrificing themselves and taking one for the team. Moving the old woman's away from the Bay's Lagoon area, would allow it to be introduced--to whoever found it--with the gators not present...but, it all needed to happen before daybreak, or they'd be out of luck. If they did nothing, the body wouldn't have sat for 5 minutes where it was, in daytime, without being discovered. The gators also decide that it'd be best if they permanently relocated the whole convocation across the channel way, over to different waters. The gators swiftly moved everything of theirs from one side of the Lagoon to the other, out of there like ghosts--they were never there!

A few days went by before the old woman's body was found, which started getting the local humans talking. People were deducing from a news stations' traffic helicopter report, which aired only a few days before the finding of the old woman's body, that a shark and whale were in fact in the area. Apparently, the traffic helicopter was just buzzing around and killing time, waiting for his turn to go live, when he saw a shark and then a whale by the shorelands in the Lagoon's Bay area. When he did get on the air, he blabbered more about seeing a whale and shark getting along, than he did about the semi-trailer that'd gone airborne, knocking down a roadside statue which then backed up the Interstate Bridge. The traffic pilot noted that he watched them because he thought they'd fight, but left knowing they weren't going to. Every local who'd watched/heard the helicopter traffic news when he reported it, thought the guy was an idiot or drunk--some people even called the station and demanded he should be fired--and everyone turned the news program off, right at that point. Once news of the old woman's body being found in the water came through, the local people still thought the traffic pilot was an airhead, but they accepted him as their own airhead. That was it! There was no need for a trial, lawyer, and certainly no attorney: the shark and whale were automatically to blame for the old woman's dying! The gators, even though being gentle, had marked up the woman's body with their teeth when moving it, but the people didn't consider them marks as anything other than from a shark; never once did the people think of the alligators.

CHAPTER 4

Wh ile the memory was still "green" (still new) of the location Motoya and Rey had fed at, over in the "new" waters, they'd agreed they should go back again very soon--like next time they were hungry soon. Rey proclaimed that "The freshest fish make the best dish!" and Motoya replied "A fish a day keeps bad luck away." The pair went on, back and forth, making up about 200 different ideas for fish slogans before finally getting back to the shoal location, noticing it was going to be a bit more difficult to cross over this time--the tide wasn't in yet. Both the shark and whale had heard horror stories about their species getting beached and they didn't want to chance that happening to them, but the drive for a lagoon muskie was too tempting, so they conceded to their stomach's desires and fought their way over the shoal, again plopping over into a nice deep body of water (compared to the other side). Little did they know, the people living around the "new" area of Ocean water had formed a militia that was just waiting to show the power of the guards. All the people were acting like they were protecting a King, just watching for a first glimpse of any trouble at the castle. That's when a man from up in a lighthouse, back across the shoal, radioed into the Lagoon Bay using his WWII 1943 RCA Marine Ship to Shore Radio: "Chance sighting! Whale... (static)...companion...last...mark...map coordinates check...(static)...beware, I repeat... (static). *Trouble. Your direct**...on the way...shark!" Then, the old Ship to Shore radios' tube blew out and the man simply faded away. However, he'd gotten his point across, and the recipient of the message used his 40 channel, 135XLR Cobra, Base Station CB Radio, relaying the message to all the Lagoon Bay town's people-- everyone had their "ears" on--which was enough to get the whole town out of bed and to the shoreline. Everyone came down to the waterfront, armed and ready. Some trigger-happy yokels saw a fin in the water and Said: "Let no wicked seeds in!" which just mustered everyone into a panic with their guns and firing blindly at the water. Whether it was poor shooting from shore or just at a bad angle is to be questioned, either way Motoya and Rey passed by it all unscathed. The shark and whale team didn't know what was happening, but they sure knew they didn't like it.

The alligators saw what was occurring from their new habitat area and Chief Gator sent a messenger gator across the channel to tell Motoya and Rey about the old woman who'd died; mentioning that the pointed blame is accredited toward the shark and whale, but that the gators were actually there when she died, and it was really nobody's fault. The messenger gator said that as a means of self-preservation, they'd wound up moving the gator colony across the Lagoon Bay, stating that they'd also tried putting the old woman's body out in the deep water as a deterrent to anyone looking, which is the people started blaming the shark and whale. The messenger said that Chief Gator hopes there's no hard feelings from the shark or whale, but that he is very sorry to have brought them into the matter. Motoya thanked the alligator for telling them the news while Rey just stayed quiet and closed her big eyes; she'd figured they were marked for death and trackers would be coming after them now, understanding too what all those people shooting at them meant. Rey suddenly shivered at thinking about their situation. Motoya's safety and freedom was gone; she was no different than an escaped convict in the eyes of the people: it was serious danger! They needed to forget about all the fish they'd come to eat and start to come up with a plan for safety. Rey tried guiding Motoya out to the deepest water in the Lagoon Bay, being she hadn't eaten to recharge, but had spent all her 106-year-old energy getting over the shoal (not to mention Motoya spent all her 66-year-old energy too). Chief Gator saw the shark and whale were very exhausted, so when they'd swam into the deep area he went over to them, giving Motoya and Rey his word that: "All the gators feel very bad for what's happened. I give you my solemn vow that we will all help the both of you in getting to safety, any way we can. Well, ladies, I bid you a fond adieu." Then, just as out of nowhere as he'd come over to them, he disappeared too.

CHAPTER 5

Stationed nearby, ashore, was a group of Ocean scientists who were well aware of Motoya and Rey's travels and activities; they'd been studying the pair for a few years already, monitoring and learning all about the odd pair-up of aquatic creatures. The scientists had "gotten a feel" of the shark and whale's daily habits and were charting the whereabouts of acts the shark and whale did for each other, but they had no idea that the local people were blaming Motoya and Rey for a woman's dying; that's when their Midland UHF/VHF Walkie Talkie, which required special FCC licensing to use, set off an SOS siren, so they 3 Ocean Scientists dropped what they were doing and ran over to it to find out was happening. Over the Walkie Talkie, someone was talking about putting a death certificate delivery group together, to hunt down the shark (specifically)-- the whale could probably be left alone. The scientists knew Motoya couldn't have killed the woman, let alone Rey--she'd have swallowed the woman whole and there'd be nothing left for evidence to know it even happened. The Ocean scientists had been out on a Watercraft vessel, just a few months earlier, making a study of actually feeding Rey and Motoya; noticing that the shark and whale, being so old, were truly missing out on 98% of the foods being put in the water for them-- understanding that the blind shark couldn't see it, and the old whale probably was following the shark at that moment (blind leading the blind). The group of scientists sympathized with the sea creatures and set out to see if they could clear the matter up with the trigger-happy gunned guard. If they couldn't, they hoped to help the 2 great fish away from the area...mostly though, the shark, as the gunned people should then leave the whale alone. Their interjection failed! Luckily, the Chief Gator kept his word and when nightfall came, he personally guided Rey and Motoya out over the shoal-assisting in aide with a nudge, tug and/ or push. Meanwhile, his gator tribe collectively went inland; taking over the entire shoreline and everything vital, to hold off or distract the people; making it impossible for anyone to get out on a boat after them.

Over the course of the next week, the scientist sympathizers rigged together a shark-sized net trap; knowing that getting the shark away from the whale wouldn't be easy, but just might save both their lives. Closely watching, the day came when Rey was preoccupied with telling some of her other whale friends about the horror she'd encountered at the land between the water, leaving Motoya safely by herself for a little while. The Ocean scientists used the unguarded moment of time as an opportunity to slip Motoya into their net trap and start to lift her out of the water--at least getting her settled on dry land so the whale couldn't see. It was a sneaky plan, but it was the only way to save her from a new threat from some specialist team the locals had felt obligated to call in (with the alligator heard attacking too and all). So, the specialists came, specifically to hunt down the shark. The sympathizer scientists had a plan sitting on the back burner too, just in case the whale came back before they'd gotten Motoya out of the water--stop, drop, and roll wouldn't help them here--they'd try tranquilizing Rey with elephant darts! It was broad daylight, there was no time to spare...no secret of night covering...daylight, anybody could be watching: good or bad!

The group of scientists were just landing Motoya ashore when I saw them, as I'd been walking along the main road due to my Suzuki Subcompact deciding it didn't want to drive all the way to an actual gas station; leaving me walking to go find one, but I took my Nikon D3200 with--didn't care if someone stole the car, but God save the camera. I happened to look over and saw 3 people down by the water, having a heck of a time reeling in their fish; being a cameraman I thought "If the fish is that big of a catch, this could be my big break: photo opportunity of a lifetime!" so I hurried and sprinted down a hill to see if I could give them a hand. It was a jaw-dropping moment, realizing they were all well over middle-aged people pulling a shark onto the dry land. I said: "Woah!" and before I even said hello, I found myself snapping off the first and only picture I'd ever take of the shark. One of them said "We're Ocean scientists, just doing a little research." There was 1 female scientist in her early 50s and 2 male scientists, one probably late 40s, the other late 60s, comprising the group. The "Kodak moment" I'd shot, was of the lady--she still had one of those 1970's fashion hairdos--just as she was sliding Motoya completely onto the dry land. They needed help or they all would have had heart attacks, as distressed as the scientists looked; I put down my camera, pulled the film and stuffed it in my pocket, then I rolled up my sleeves and dove in to help move the shark up and around an embankment to a more sloped area of the yard. I asked, "Where are we going with this fish?" to which one of the male scientists replied by pointing all the way up the yard's hill slope to an old shack, leaving me to question his sanity (not to mention the other 2's), but I said "O.K.! Let's...let's get going then." Sure enough, as we were heaving the great fish up, up and away, toward the shack, I saw my camera get eaten by the tides' current--at least I had my film. While resting with the fish only 1/4 of the way up the hill's sloped yard, I noticed the grass was quite healthy, and that if we wetted it under her it might make moving the fish slide easier--sharks having skin, not scales--using her body's design to our advantage. I said "Hold on! Let's work smarter, not harder...get me a bucket of water. Let's make an uphill Slip 'N' Slide," so one of the men fetched a bucket and poured it under Motoya as I gave her a nudge and she scooted herself forward; after 2 more buckets she was scooching herself without the need to be nudged; she just followed the path of the water that had whetted the lawn. Like a dog that's just learned a new trick, she was showing off her intelligence to us. The scientists weren't completely surprised and said "As you can see, this fish is very special. We've been studying her for 6 years...would you believe she's blind too." I said "Get out of here! Really...really?!" The 3 let out a resounding cry of "Yes!" I figured out the shark's name in talking to them more, and that I was the first person they'd even discussed anything of their Motoya work with--outside of each other that is. One of the male scientists quickly grabbed a pair of binoculars as if a tornado was coming and said, "Rey's back!" I didn't know what Rey was yet, but the 2 other scientists shivered and got goosebumps, acting like they'd seen a ghost and Motoya just started moving like she was back in the water swimming.

CHAPTER 6

Rey, unable to find Motoya after returning from her brief time out with the other whales (gossiping time), believed she must've smelled a fish nearby and went to find it, being there was no evidence to assume otherwise. The longer that time passed, Rey thought Motoya must have gotten lost out there somewhere. She started to feel like an idiot for not going looking for Motoya before that moment, knowing darned well that for the last 40 years Motoya hadn't had any vision. Rey was tired and exhausted, but she looked day and night, night and day...2 weeks went by when she finally concluded that wherever Motoya was, it had to be someplace nearby--little could she know how near though. She started thinking that maybe Motoya went senile, on top of being blind, and just maybe she'd tried to find her way over the shoal and got...God forbid the thought...stuck! Like a racehorse gone crazy, Rey pushed her 106-year-old body's heart to the max, making it to the shoal and clearing herself over it like it was the Summer Olympic high jump--she went over it back first, perfect form. Something must've let loose in Rey's head, as she splashed the Lagoon Bay's water to kingdom come, making it as noisy as possible, like a "I'm here, I'm here" call splash: no Motoya response. Chief Gator heard Rey's calls of exhausted discouragement "Where...are you? Where, where are you Mo... a?" He was very concerned now, thinking that maybe the shark hunters did indeed track her down and maybe they were following right behind Rey--and they would be too. The Lagoon people heard the splash, got radio confirmation from the lighthouse about it being a whale, and they naturally assumed the shark was there with her too...though the specialists were docked and waiting, way across the Lagoon with their cheap Coast Guard Cutter, the Holly Muck, which they'd got at auction because the USCG's Captain had blown the motor on it while speeding in Canada, so it was either salvage it or auction it; the specialists got it for 1, very badly tarnished, penny. Rey, still unable to find Motoya, took a solemn pledge to protect the Bay from intruders, hoping in some way that she'd be protecting Motoya in the long run--she knew her back wasn't going to let her leave the Bay ever again either: broken! Rey started to hum Lean on Me, crying more unanswered tears than an unemployed man who doesn't have a job to feed his hungry baby, or house his family.

CHAPTER 7

Meanwhile, back on dry land at the shack, I really started wondering why the grass was actually the greenest, prettiest I'd ever come across, so I asked one of the scientists what they were feeding it...sorry I can't give you more details on that part; it's now a trade secret and why I have lots of money, however, I can say we'll come back to talk about money later in the story. At the shack Motoya was being sprayed with an industrial type of garden hose--certainly, not very common in those days. Motoya put her head to my hand, like a dog wanting to be petted, so I gave her a few as I said, asking anyone who'd answer, "Her will is her own!?" to which the female scientist said, "It sure is, Brother." I swear, that shark took fondly to me, quicker than any girlfriend I'd ever had, and in the shark's case she meant it. The scientists all went to open 2 separate sets of cellar doors, each on opposite ends of the shack, leaving me standing alone with Motoya--

obviously they all trusted the shark, but even more so they trusted me. My mind wondered: "Was I being tested? No, wait...was I going to become shark food?" Motoya turned in the direction of the cellar door on the side of the shack with a ramp that would allow for cart use in bringing things up or down from the shack cellar, while the other door had a set of stairs going inside. The scientists had whetted the ramp and were ready for me to guide Motoya over, so she could slide inside. I felt like we were rebels, but with a cause! In the heat of the moment, as I got Motoya lined up with the ramp down into the cellar, I took a moment to talk to her like a daughter and told her "I love you!" She didn't hesitate to nudge my hand before sliding her way down into the cellar. "What was happening to me...was the heat making me loopy...I helped strangers pull an Ocean shark, just to hide it in their cellar...I lost my camera and... hey that's right, I have film...film with proof to mail in...my big break...it's...it's going to go to National Geographic."

The scientists came up from the cellar, knowing nothing about my private talk with Motoya-- which is how I kept it too--and told me the ugly truth; that we had moved Motoya to the cellar for her own good, or she would've been killed. Before I could ask any questions, I looked over at Motoya, just down in the cellar safe room from me; she was looking right in my direction, smiling out to me with her big, beautiful, blind eyes and was nodding her head at me...hand on the bible, I swore she actually said to me: "I shall obey." I've never been more certain about my life, as I was in that mere second; the shark chose me, trusted me, she wanted me to tell her story. Immediately, I started to write her story down on a few scraps of paper laying around and using a pen that must've been used by a leftie for a while (the roller tip had taken a directional curve) before using it to write with. I went around asking for as much information as the scientists would indulge me in from their last

6 years of researching Motoya.

As I started writing, all the scientists chimed in with facts and statistics, but I knew Motoya wanted me to tell the story as if to show it happening, not just in pie graphs and Oceanographic terms. So, I stole their stupid logbook and went into the cellar to read it to Motoya, getting to the bottom of the actual story like any good reporter should. Motoya really got excited when I said things about Rey, then I realized she wanted me to go get her Rey, or some news about her. I told her that 1 of the scientists had a pair of binoculars, so I'd borrow them and go walk down by the ocean to look for her. It was all I could think of doing, but if I'd known what was going to happen soon after I'd said that to Motoya, I would have said get in the boat with me Mot (that was my nickname for her), we got a war to win! The 2 separate sets of cellar doors were mandatory for 2 means of egress, in case of fire

(fire exits). The floor drains in the cellar safe room became a means to cycle out dirty water with clean, running a sump-pump periodically to cycle out dirty water and bringing in the fresh ocean water by reversing a dredge pump. The safe room cellar had a few wooden shelving units where food was kept for storage, but now would have Motoya's toys--yes, she was much like a dolphin with her toys--and "good girl" snack treats--she was rewarded often. There was an original Edison lightbulb still burning strong in a pull chain light fixture (though the chain was a string). If you came out of the ramped side of the safe room cellar too fast and turned left, you could slip right down the sloped yard, winding up rolling till you got to the Ocean, which was good for a boat launch I devised; however, the dangerous part still became how steep that yard got and in such a hurry. Being blind, Motoya couldn't have seen any of that or the geography layout, but what happened soon after made me believe that she somehow could distinguish light from total darkness. Her, getting light shining in her eyes while above sea level (on land) allowed it to "hit different," compared to the little bit of light that penetrates the depths of the dark Ocean, not getting down as far as people assume, direct radiant light vs penetrative light.

CHAPTER 8

Narrator Break, present time: "Now, just coming back to the shack's location 26 years later, all those scientist sympathizers have long since passed away and from what I've heard from town folk, Motoya is looked at as a symbol of hope and freedom from a past long gone by. The shack's cellar is a safe room, well, let's just say it's just as safe as it ever was; the shack really wasn't constructed by engineers, so the fact that it's still standing at all is a miracle. When I first placed my feet on the roadside soil here, I was just 18 years old, looking to get published, but now I'm 43 and retracing my past, righting the things I can along the way. Everything is everything."

CHAPTER 9

I'd been staying with the scientists for a whole day already and really needed to continue onward to get gas and move my car off the road, getting on my way. I told Motoya I had a good feeling about her story and told her I just needed to rewrite the paper into a final copy, to which she agreed--knowing I was her friend and wouldn't lie about her. I'd thoroughly believed, her blindness must've caused her other senses (smell, taste, hear, feel, etc.) to heighten, going into unprecedented levels. It was the only way for me to make sense of why she, like a well-trained dog, was able to get me to understand her wants and desires. She had a way of making it known, to me, that she "Wanted to know, what's going on," and that she wanted me to keep her posted on things. I couldn't stay with her forever, and I needed to tell her that. I petted her and said, "They can't hurt you now," based on what I'd learned about people with a ship that were specifically hired in trying to hunt her down, out in the Ocean waters. I stayed the night at the shack, listening to 1 of the scientists doing landmass equations in his dreams--it was a long night. I left the next afternoon, throwing Motoya a treat (as one would to a dog) as I passed by her safe room cellar on my way. The scientists gave me a milk jug filled with fuel for my car, taken from the generator's large gas can, so I could at least get my car to the next filling station. I went and got gas, had the 1 picture developed quickly at a place called 5 Minute Photo, went to a diner and rewrote the Motoya story while eating lunch, then mailed off the article at the local USPS on my way out of Town, going home.

At once, after I'd mailed the Motoya picture with her story to National Geographic, telling them every detail I could of the rescue-- almost everything, being I didn't mention her being blamed for an old woman dying elsewhere part--they sent me a free year's subscription to the magazine and offered me a job photographing livestock in the Bitanga Congo. I kept a close eye out for any news reports, through television and radio, from anywhere in the vicinity of where Motoya was shacked up. And so it happened, a few weeks later the nearby Lagoon Bay was reporting about an Orca whale attack. It was all the buzz on the airwaves, broadcast over most of the Southern Ocean's area. Apparently, men with guns in cigar boats came speeding into the Bay, along with the old USCG cutter Holly Muck, dropping anchor right over to the area where the alligators and Rey were. The manipulative Captain of the Holly Muck had hired the cigar boats to spy on the waters for him, so once the whale was known to be there, the shark must be too if the whale hadn't left yet. He told his hired vessels a small rumor that: "A serpent shark with a deadly stinger is in these waters. It goes out looking for spots along the shoreline where wildflowers grow, so's to catch an unsuspecting person in their surprise. The shark's stinger releases a deadly poison into the waters, which then the local people drink and use that water; dying like the old woman had. "It was a direct "bullet of fear," meant to keep the men well motivated to find the shark first! Whoever got him some shark news would win a large percent of an ownership claim in his ship; it was a way for him to avoid paying much, if any of the taxes himself (the taxes were well more than the ship was worth).

CHAPTER 10

Chief Gator sent his entire division, including going himself too, out to defend the front of the waterway. On his way over, passing Rey, he stated: "See you on the sunny side. They aren't here to have any discussions." Across the Lagoon Bay the locals cocked guns by the dozens *Click, Slam, Chang, ting* then, the firing commenced; horrible amounts of gunfire were aimed and fired at the water--which is actually against the 10 Commandments of Firearm Safety: rule no.8--but it was the big ship and cigar boat gunners that got a real bead on the gators; dropping 1/4 of the gators faction before it could make any real advance onto the shoreline, which then the locals were well ready for what came. Motoya started to see red in anger and came rushing toward the water top, blowing a massive water spout out of her blowhole, so big it looked almost like a mini-A-bomb...the captain staring directly into Rey's right eye in disbelief as she surfaced. The captain turned his head, drew out his revolver, aimed directly at the back of Chief Gators' head, and with a *Kaboom* Rey watched her gator comrade fade away into red oblivion. That Captain's action was a new definition of "low down and dirty!" The captain of the cutter turned his head back to look directly into Rey's big eye again...no words did he say, he just spit. All the remaining alligators and the Orca whale were energized, now with vengeance (not unlike the locals, who'd felt the same about the shark) only in mind for whatever their cause--right or wrong-- and Rey knew it was her time to shine.

The gators tried their best to fend off cigar boats and the guns kept firing, but the gators had made some progress at the far end of the shore bank, where the action wasn't anything. Some of the smaller boats started noticing what was going on and left to head over to the far end. Anger was in Rey's every muscle, plus she was still under the belief that Motoya was somewhere nearby and defenseless...with all the brutes around that wasn't a good feeling. Rey started raving into a madness that no one has seen since maybe Moby Dick, she homed in on the Holly Muck, particularly, and let out a bellow sounding like "Fishmonger!" as she barreled toward the ship; ramming it and causing the manipulative Captain to fall overboard into "the drink." Rey laughed at seeing him fall and said "Rub-a-dub, Captain." She continued in her rage, tossing giant waves of water and flipping cigar boats over with her monstrous tail, yelling "Where's my friend!?" to anyone who could hear her--she demanded answers.

    The people on land and on the ship got very angry at Rey. They started acting like her knocking the captain into the drink (water) was as if she'd killed their King while he was sleeping, so they began to march forward at her, guns blazing, in a full-scale attack on the whale. The cigar boat people couldn't do much but watch, as most of their boats were overturned by the whale's great tail splashings, and left them asking themselves: "What the hockey is that Orca doing? That lying Captain said, "We're here for a shark, yet there isn't a shark in these waters!" The cigar boat people figured the chance to own part in a beat up old USCG cutter wasn't worth it anyway, so they helped each other right their boats and split the area fast; leaving the captain and his crew on the ship and the land people to figure their mess out. The captain finally made it ashore, huffing and puffing from swimming. Once He got the land people to stop firing, he summoned his ship to come pick him up. The first thing he did, once gotten back on the ship, was fire his Boatswain's Mate for not checking on him. He pushed the ex-Boatswain's Mate right over the starboard side of the ship, landing the man down by some mad gators, then the captain just walked away silently, passing through the quarterdeck, and finally shutting himself in his cabin to draw up a plan.

Rey continued tossing water around till nightfall, but the land people and the ship's crew weren't sure why the captain was so obsessed over a whale, being there hadn't been any sign of a shark with it all day; surely with all of the shooting and splashing and alligator action no shark was just going to come swimming in now--either it was there, or it wasn't. The captain emerged from his cabin, all changed into dry clothing and wearing a very Napoleonic style hat, which got everyone's attention--even from those on shoreline--when he proceeded to read a mandate he'd declared: "Punishment to any and all wildlife that stands in the way of apprehending the shark." Note: By the word punish, what the captain really meant was kill, as wounded animals (gators, angry whales, anything) are even more dangerous than uninjured ones. Also note: Whale killing (A.K.A. whaling) went out of style in the early 1900s, so the despicably evil act the captain was attempting to perform is criminal...just saying.

CHAPTER 11

The manipulative captain had become fed-up with watching the Orca tossing everything around--like a kid who doesn't want a bath in a bathtub full of toys--so he called his mother, hoping she'd reaffirm him in his actions. His mother was third cousin to some shirttail relative of some member of Parliament, plus she was a notary public with a rubber stamp; he felt like he had an official seal of approval for his destructive actions if he got her involved in his making decisions. The captain told his mother the issue he'd been having with the whale, so together they worked out a plan, even giving it a special codename. As soon as his mother said adieu, the call was over, and he hung up the phone and spit. During the time of the phone call, all 3 of the Scientist sympathizers had arrived at the Lagoon Bay shoreline. They'd heard there was a ruckus with an Orca whale there and knew it must be Rey, so they came to see if they could stop the madness.

At first, it seemed like they might be able to, as the locals at the shoreline mentioned they were tired of wrestling alligators and gave up on the shark they wanted even being there anyway--they all wanted to go to bed, really. Of course, Captain Napoleonic hat returned to his command deck and grabbed a megaphone, causing all his men to stand at attention while waiting for his next order. The captain didn't let them down, speaking through the megaphone not only to his crew but the locals on the shore as well, giving the commanding speech: "Gentlemen, we are at war! As once in history, when an enemy was too much for a frontal attack, the Ambassador sent dudes marching through Poland to attack Denmark. So shall we too be just as well thought out of an army, only at Sea." At least 2 of the seamen looked lost at each other, wondering what the captain was driving at, saying to each other "Just an army passing through...no biggie." After a long, little while of silence, the men, in perfect unison, asked "What's the plan Captain?" The captain looked up at the moon and realized it was a Supermoon, then looked out at his crew and yelled a reply through his megaphone: "The Ambassador is back!" One of the scientists was once appointed as a consulate in Canada, realizing that that ship Captain was referring to an old model of cannon, which they'd used to fire off full of candy on special days (like Boxing Day) just for parade fun--what would be loaded in the captains' cannon wasn't any good for parade fun though. The scientist lost his cool and yelled back to the captain: "The Devil! How dare you infuse your morbidity on an American water vessel-- even if it is beaten to a pulp? Scoundrel!" The mischievous Captain sent some men out in a rescue boat to fetch him the shouting scientist, which caused the 2 other scientist sympathizers to do the whole "Keep your filthy hands off him!" thing. The 3 sympathizer scientists were brought out to the ship and put in a quarterdeck room for a special interrogative session by a man who was known as an E-2 non-rate, but none of the 3 scientists came back out of the room when the man known as E-2 non-rate returned. The man gave the captain an oddly disconcerting look and nonchalantly left with the ships' lifeboat, not just boating to the shore, he was leaving the area absolutely.

There were 3 large caliber Ambassador cannons stationed aboard the old cutter Holly Muck: one on the stern, one on the bow and one down in the ship's cargo bay. The captain ordered that they all be brought to the main deck and be placed 10ft apart from each other, as well as loaded and ready. The men didn't want to disappoint, so they loaded the cannons with more iron ore properties and gunpowder than Godly imaginable--it was an overcharged city!

CHAPTER 12

And so, the captain called Operation Ambassador into effect; all shipmates got to their assigned posts and duties. The ship made an adjusted maneuver, allowing its rudder to turn counterclockwise to come around the old whales' left side in a surprise attack strategy. Like Hamlet calling out Polonius, the captain called out the giant Orca whale. He looked her dead in the left eye, and with a sinister grin commanded his men to "Fire at will!" When the first Ambassador went off, the overcharge being so great, the entire cannon exploded as it fired; throwing shrapnel iron in every direction and turning 1/3 of the shipmates into ghosts in a moment's time. The first cannon backfiring explosion triggered the second one into going off automatically, which also blew itself up sky high into pieces, the second triggering the third in the chain reaction; all the ship's crew and the ship itself were done for; the catastrophic reaction of bad planning. As the unholy succession of firings and exploding ended, the remains of the ship and crew were sent to the bottom of the Ocean Bay, sadly taking the great whale down with it. Each cannon firing had hit its intended mark on the whale's body. Witnesses say the cannon shot her with a pattern like the 3 corners of a triangle; causing the whale to blow up like a Hawaiian Volcano that's in season. The fish sank like a rock! The people began to panic at the inland shoreline, not knowing what to do and knew they were all going to have the whales' image burned into their subconscious minds for eternity. For those on land who'd attacked the whale, it was futile to lie to themselves, they'd have it worse than the folks who'd left, quit, and/or gave up with no shark present anyhow. Some cameramen from the Associates Digest Research Firm (ADRF) got a few "hunters" on record saying "Oh God! God! It would've been better to have waited for evolution to take her fate, compared to what we did that day. We never even found the shark!" It's also stated that God responded to them and said, "Stop whining!" so only the active participants can/could hear--and they will live long, long, long lives.

Miraculously, the E-2 non-rate must have sympathized with the scientists who, for whatever reasons didn't (or couldn't) get off the ship that went down. He had taken all their Id's with when he'd left on the lifeboat. So, knowing they were innocent in the whaling incident--he wasn't far enough away from the general area, so kept hearing from people about how a ship had gone down with the whale--he felt it his duty to somehow let their family find out of their disappearance; going back to the scene and gradually letting the Id's float into the shore near where the ship went down. The police started investigating the occurrence during daylight and were able to gather from locals who were there that the Id's matched the 3 scientists that were taken to the ship. The police could only find 1 family member, who happened to be the son of the scientist sympathizer who owned the shack, so they called and alerted him that the 3 had

99.999% surely perished. The son, coming in from an apartment for men at the state line, packed up all his belongings in a suitcase, told the landlord he was leaving and to keep the deposit (left the place filthy), laughing as he got in his car. Stopping at a gas station for canned foods and cereal while on his way to the shack, he stole the then latest issue of National geographic--he only wanted to picture of Aboriginal tribes--which happened to be the one with my shark picture and story printed in it--though he didn't know that then. He'd learn about the shark after reading the article that night, unbelieving, but then finding her in the cellar.

CHAPTER 13

About 4 months went by and I was at home, folding laundry after taking a shower, when a police report of 3 missing scientists, whose Id's had washed up on shore near the Lagoon Bay, confirmed that they were in fact the same people being brought up from the cutter ship remains--theirs were also the only remains ever recovered! Apparently, the rest of the ship was decimated, but the room where they'd been held was classified as a fireproof and bulletproof safe room. Investigators learned, as it turned out, that the door was locked and barred shut at the handle outside, using a non-descript length of pipe, thus, keeping it from opening--no evidence of foul play was discovered though. I rushed to throw on some clothing, grabbed all the food from my freezer and fridge headed straight out for the shack. "God help her!" I prayed, not knowing the scientist's son would be there when I arrived, or the derelict conditions everything fell into his hands; the prayer would've been much more involved, had I known.

Arriving at the shack, I ran to the cellar and found the water too low and Motoya barely holding on--truthfully, I didn't think she would still be alive. I ran down into the cellar and turned on the sump pump, wondering why that hadn't been running at least, then took a moment to pet her and tell her "Everything's alright now, I got this!" as I saw the light of life come back into her blind eyes...the hose for fresh Ocean water from the reverse dredging was tossed into the yard, so I rushed to get it, fired up the generator (pumping fresh water into the cellar) and ran back to my car to get Motoya something to eat from all the fridge and freezer food I'd brought. I got her upright and breathing ok again, then had to hand feed her small pieces of food; making it easier to eat and digest. That's when I saw that there was another car pulling in the shacks' driveway, so I'd assumed the neighbor or police might be wondering who's here with the scientists all gone bye-bye. I was all set for answering that question, being my article was by then printed in National Geographic, which, with the picture I'd taken and the communications I'd quoted directly from all 3 scientists, would prove I'd been there before and/or that maybe I was given permission by them, for coming back anytime I'd like and continuing the story. That's not who pulled in though, instead it was a man who broke Motoya's divine inner peace and solitude when she heard him coming...dammit; in a way an animal can explain it to you. I told her whatever was coming, I'd handle it--seemed to help calm her some. Before the man came to encounter me, he had to hide a few things, which took him a few minutes, as he'd thought I was the police or a neighbor too--had to be the first time anyone even came there, since he'd arrived. I was telling Motoya Rey had fallen to a cause...she was gone...all the scientists perished as well...but not in vain, that Rey's fighting to defend the alligators was noble, as if she believed in "something after death," which helped Motoya understand that Rey must've been defending as a way of watching out for her too--though she was blind, she could clearly see purpose. I told her that the scientists had gone to try to stop the ship and locals from shooting her, but Motoya already knew that as they'd told her they were going before they left. I repeated to her what 1 of the scientists had told me: "There is a lesson to be learned with everything that occurs." I petted her and said "There, there, Rey's act was an act of salvation. She knew they'd kill her but didn't think twice to defend her shark and alligator friends." The speech was almost a soliloquist prayer to Motoya's ears, and she came to a conclusion, right then and there, that she'd have to get back in the water to pay respects to Rey's final resting place; knowing too, she'd never get back out to the water without my help--her thin and weakened state was making its presence more and more. When I was telling her "You'll never make it out there if you go; It's surely final surrender! However, I won't hesitate to help, because, like I said before, I love you." She bowed, smiled and nodded and was just about to come forward to the ramp way up, when the new owner of the shack, Mr. Scientists Son, apprehensively met me at the cellar door. I could see Motoya was shaking, scared, and the water was reflecting that feeling around her.

CHAPTER 14

Turning to greet the man, he squinted his eyes at me, hard and harsh, when he realized I wasn't a cop, then he got mean and verbally argumentative with me, accusing me of trespassing and read me the riot act. He was the kind of guy that liked to speak to you, instead of to you, but did it while keeping one hand on his gun holster. I was appalled just looking at the guy! I told him who I was and that before he shunned anyone, maybe he ought to look up the DNR's rules of having a wild shark captive in their basement-- that shut him up, for a minute anyway. He said: "If you knew about how all the water works around here, you must be that jerk who took a picture of my shark and got famous for printing a fable story!" Out from back pocket he pulled a National Geographic magazine and threw it on the ground by my feet in anger, growling: "Your tale was trash and there weren't any Aborigines' pictures printed in the magazine either!" I didn't reply to his criticisms, instead I tried to reason with the man about allowing me to be the director of the sharks' care, if not there then someplace else more accommodating to her, as it was plain to see she wasn't getting fed enough and was drying out--the scientists son needed to dry out too, in my opinion. The shack was not in good repair, so I thought maybe he'd agree, once he came to his senses, but he never did either. Instead, the man freaked out on me for giving the fish new water, saying how: "That fish is my golden ticket to a first-place taxidermy mount! " I was appalled and that's when Motoya let out a whine of disparity (the sound broke barriers that only Angels have been able to cross). He didn't feel any remorse about his sinful actions, not taking care of the shark--he meant to starve her to death, so he could have the thinnest shark mount ever. I couldn't do much about it, so I decided to come back when nightfall came, to sneak and hide in Motoya's room. It was the son's property now, so if he was on his last nerves and tired of answering my questions, even after telling me to "Get lost and don't come back!" and me not going, he really could have me arrested; however, that wouldn't help Motoya out, so I picked up the National geographic magazine and set it on a wooden shelf, just inside the cellar door, glaring over my shoulder at the shack owner the whole time as I walked away and left.

CHAPTER 15

Coming back that night, I parked my car down the road right where I'd run out of gas before, walking over to the shack from there to stay unnoticed, then snuck down into the cellar. I brought Motoya and myself a few hard-boiled eggs, so we'd have energy for the plan I was crafting. The reality was that the shark's life was chaos in that cellar, maybe more now than ever, but she never belonged there in the first place. I fed Motoya an egg and rested with her, petting her and working on a plan to get her out of there. In her exhaustion, she snuggled my hand and finally went to sleep. I quietly swore to her, so as not to wake her, that she'd see the green-green grass and her Ocean home once again--creating a viable escape plan for the shark, only doing it all on my own (no sympathizer scientists this time to help move her back to the water). Her safe room mind as well have been in England, vs where it really was, being she was so weak it wasn't just a quick and easy thing to guide her anywhere...then again, maybe.... Thinking about using objects around the cellar: a fish in a crate, the Nat. Geo. magazine, the pull-string light fixture, wooden shelving, I was turning out the old Edison bulb in the cellar, when suddenly a plan for helping Motoya escape at first light of dawn hit me.

Early dawn came and I opened the cellar door with the ramp a few inches; just enough to get some light in, but not to draw attention. The bit of sunlight that pierced its way into the cellar was very encouraging, so I said to Motoya: "Elijah's light is upon us, giving us a guiding way now." With that, I began by unscrewing the Edison lightbulb from the light fixture, placing it on a nearby countertop, then pulled down the light fixture while trying to break the pull-string from it. Motoya must've been able to see light and dark, even though she was blind, as she started moving herself toward the sunlight that was coming into the cellar. Next, I took the fish from the crate and tied the pull-string around it, allowing me to use it as one would a carrot to guide a horse. The crate fish was a Bass, but it was obviously being grown in captivity so that the shack owner could lie about it as a naturally caught prize sized fish. I figured too, that he was getting joy from feeding it in front of Motoya, while not feeding her: very cruel. I finished up and put the fish's crate back, then got in front of Motoya while dragging the fish on a sting and guided her right up to the top of the ramp, opening the door wide at the top, very slowly, while watching for any sign of the shack owner. I left the fish on the ground, just outside the cellar with the ramp, then told Motoya to wait, as I was going to quickly peek out the opposite side cellar door; just seeing that the coast was clear all around before making a break for it. Of course, the moment I stepped away, Motoya took the liberty to scootch herself out the door and eat the bass fish I'd rigged up--jeez! I couldn't blame her though.

Climbing the stairs at the other cellar door, I slowly opened it about an inch, but that was enough for the mean owner to see me: he was standing right there, waiting. He said: "I expected your betrayal! My intentions aren't like yours, now you..." I shut the door on him and moved out of the way quickly, knowing he meant "die," so I was sure he had bad intentions and his gun too. There was no way he knew Motoya was as good as home free by that point anyway; she was already just outside the cellar, so if she turned left and got a little push, she would slide downhill over the very overgrown and morning dew covered lawn, easily flowing herself into the Ocean at the bottom. She'd already seen light from darkness, so she didn't need me guiding her in that last foot's distance anymore anyway. She was purely just waiting for me like an obedient dog staying when commanded to.

The owner of the shack lunged through the door, believing he'd be slamming it into me; trying to knock me down or injure me with it. He yelled: "Not on my watch!" at me as he barreled in so hard and fast, but I'd moved so there was nothing to stop his forward momentum, causing him to come flying into the cellar right past me and falling down the staircase headfirst; thwacking his head into the cement floor at the bottom. The sound of *thwack* echoed through the mostly empty cellar area. The man started to get up to his hands and knees, trying to reach into his holster for his .45/410 pistol called The Judge, surely meaning to shoot it at me, so I jumped over him from up on the last stair and landed my weight down onto his hand; causing him to drop in pain again for a moment. Looking at the man's head, I saw he had sustained a serious looking injury from smacking into the floor like that...but I'm no doctor. The man was putting his hand onto the lower stair tread for leverage and pulling himself up when he looked and saw Motoya across the cellar, out to the top of the ramps' landing, so he drew his pistol and cocked the hammer. I saw what he was doing, and I kicked him, which in my defense isn't what made the gun fire, but it sure rearranged his aim; the man collapsed onto the staircase and stopped moving--he was dead. He could stay there dead on the staircase too, for all I cared, as I realized the guns' firing scared Motoya into jumping away from the cellar doorway landing; between her weight and size as a natural force, the yard's slope trajectory took over the rest (like something put on autopilot) and turned the dew-covered grass into a giant Slip 'N' Slide for her, leading right into the Ocean at the end. I rushed over and saw her sailing down the hill when she was about 3/4 of the way to the end; the exit method of the plan had worked. All I could do was yell out: "Wee! Way to go Motoya!" and cheer her on. Watching closely, the yards' end boat launch part was coming up, so I crossed my fingers, watching that the transcendence to Ocean went smoothly. Motoya stopped just at the end before the water, allowing me time to run down and catch up with her; like she was suddenly calling a meeting to make sure we were on the same page with everything. Really, it was a moment to say goodbye, because if the gun firing hadn't scared her, we'd have said it at the hilltop before she went sliding down. I gave her a big hug and told her that

I loved her, making the heart shape with both my hands, only this time I put them on her to feel, so she was ok then. As she swam away, I waved and held up "Love!" She was back where she belonged, being guided only by her inner moonlight; at long last, she was back home.

CHAPTER 16

I never did tell the police about the guy who tried to shoot me, or that he was laying in his cellar; telling them would have led me to having to explain the shark rescue, probably all the way to the beginning when the Ocean scientists were alive, also why it'd brought me back there again during the night. From the looks of things, now coming back here 26 years later, the local community doesn't seem to acknowledge the guy was ever there at the shack anyway. A few days after I'd helped Motoya escape and had gone back home myself, leaving the state, I saw a National News report about a Guiness Book of Records aged shark in the community recreation waters around there--sense then, being redeveloped into the White Sands Beachfront Properties, Inc. Anyway, the news was interviewing a local historian who'd suggested that the shark was about 70 years in age, recommending that the city should put the shark in its museum; accrediting that she would become a tourist attraction, because there was something "special" about their community waters that would lead to life longevity. He went on to self-promote his area by saying: "Of course, I can confirm that there are great human benefits in the water here too!" I could already see the City and Town's population booming, much like it had in Waukesha, Wisconsin; back when their spring water was believed to cure what ailed folks, in the early part of the 1900s. Motoya's accused past with the woman who passed away was suddenly irrelevant to the locals, as the people turned the long-life shark into a community celebrity; starting a yearly classic car parade to commemorate her, hanging banners and streamers and special lights, even naming their firework show after her! Finding that out, I instantly felt 1,000 of Cupid's love arrows hit my heart and I cried.

I knew Motoya had made her peace in visiting

the area of her friend Rey too. When the locals found Motoya's body, it started them into checking the waters for more amazingly aged fish (hoping to find living ones) and discovering only that an original Edison lightbulb was perfectly positioned, set into and standing atop a freshly covered sand mound underwater. The news anchor had jokingly commented that it looked like when someone puts a flower at another's gravesite--how right they were though! I've spent the last 26 years attempting to guess how that shark snuck the lightbulb out of the safe room with her, but my ceasing to capitulate to a wrong idea has finally ended. Finding the answer to the perplexing question is part of what's brought me back here all these years later--though that's a whole different topic of another story, which I haven't finished writing, meaning life. There's an old joke about 2 grave diggers in the church cemetery; one telling the other that the hole "...needs to be wider," the other replying back that "the plot thickens." There's also a local story, though I don't remember the whole thing, where 2 grave diggers are arguing at the church cemetery, fighting over a skull while joking to each other about the building--it's no prize is my guess--and who's not allowed to be buried in its graveyard, let alone even have a funeral there. I made my millions in the last 26 years, simply recreating the old scientist's recipe for lawn food and modifying the special hoses for applying it, so that they're easy enough even a child can use them. A new shade of green was added to the color spectrum due to the results of my formula...again trade secret...but I'll spill this detail; it involves water. My company is called Lawn Green, so people know me by the name Lawn Green King. I've just given the local Church and the City's Mayor the biggest contributions this Town has ever seen (and probably ever will). The mayor's brother is an Ordained Minister over at the church. Both locations are supplying funding for the Museum to even exist. Guess who's just gotten a "honorary plot of nobility," specially opened at the Church's Cemetery?!

--The End--

KEN AND PEACHES

CHAPTER 1

Ken and Peaches are an interracial couple; she's black, he's white. They'd heard about a small town, known as a "for building" town, where 100 years ago a racial equality activist named John Lynch had lived. The story was that John Lynch had come from a white family; however, unlike the others in his family, and even the town, he was helping people of color (black) learn how to read and write; giving them a basic education. The town's folk grew furious at John Lynch, noticing Negro people they'd employed--putting them to work in forced labor camps--started showing signs of having educational roots. Up till that point, the negro worker would've responded "Yesh sur" to a given command; but with some ABC's and 123's in their repertoire, they'd started answering commands with "Yes Sir," and asking follow-up questions and/or starting conversations like: "Was there anything else you'd like today Sir?" or jovially saying

"Hey, Mrs. such-and-such, I've just read the book (whatever the latest new book of the times was) and found it wonderful. Reads like that can really motivate a person to write a novel themselves." Even Mr. Lynch's own household grew intolerant towards his allowing Negro folk under their house roof! Unanimously, the town got together and hung John Lynch, trying to make an example of him; however, his educational teachings lived on. Peaches' Mother was the granddaughter of someone who Mr. Lynch had taught to read and write, very well, and had become a high profiled author in her day. Peaches and Ken had driven about two hours to reach the old "for building" town, wanting to pay their respects to the home of the honorable deceased local hero.

CHAPTER 2

Peaches is a very dark-haired woman who's always playing around with its appearance, changing it up every month. Ken always notices her hairstyle changes, so compliments Peaches on everyone--he believes no matter what she does to her hair, or what she wears (or doesn't wear), she always looks like a Princess. When Ken first met Peaches, he was an outsourced repair man, hired to fix a plumbing issue, and working for the apartment landlord where Peaches lived. Apparently, someone had rigged a Moen faucet to an outside garden hose, running it up to her apartment through a window, and then adapted it to Peaches' kitchen sink; instead of repairing the water feed lines below the sink cabinet. When Ken knocked on Peaches' apartment door (being there wasn't a doorbell buzzer) she answered wearing only a bath towel, because the abusive "person"--he was just a monster--she'd been seeing, had just taken all her clothes and dumped her; leaving

Peaches with only: a bath towel (which she was wrapped in), a wet bath mat, and a shower curtain. Peaches' now ex-boyfriend had just broken-up with her, while she was showering, right before Ken arrived to do the faucet repair work. Where Peaches' ex took off with the laundry is still unknown. Before Ken could focus on the repair job he'd been sent to do, his and Peaches' eyes met; locking each other's glances with unrestricted sparkles (they were both seeing stars), and time seemed to stand still--it was just too magical for words. Ken was immediately concerned that Peaches might catch cold, being dressed in only a towel, so he ran out to his truck to fetch her some extra clothes he'd kept on hand, then quickly brought them back to her. Peaches put on Ken's: sweatshirt, blue jeans, and a pair of Under Armor sneakers, to which Ken stated, "There has never been a Princess so beautiful as you!" Before Ken finished the faucet repair work, Peaches and he were engaged . . . though some might say, like twin-flames, they were already married in time, the soul's commitment between two people is worth more than any saying of "I do" in front of some Clergy Man/Woman. Peaches started phoning ahead for a pizza to be picked up on their way home, because she wasn't going to need to live in the poverty laden apartment any longer. She was going to be living with Ken now, in a real home, full of real love (though love is too small a word for what they had together), as her new life of fiancé had started.

About the moment Ken and Peaches were leaving the apartment forever, black smoke came pouring into it from a cracked window in the back bedroom. The smoke, as it turned out, was being sent into the apartment by Peaches' mental-case ex-boyfriend. Peaches' ex was a racist; believing in black with black only and didn't know someone besides Peaches was even at the apartment, till catching a glimpse of Ken holding the passenger side door of his truck open for Peaches, then driving off together. Peaches' ex yelled out in a fury "That WHITE (expletive)!" Apparently, Peaches' crazy ex-boyfriend was trying to smoke her out of the apartment, planning to put her mostly nude (knowing he'd taken her laundry, leaving nothing to wear) and running into the street, making her a humiliating show for public display. Peaches put 2+2 together, figuring out what the ex was trying to do to her, which drove her even closer to Ken--as if there were such a thing as closer than what Peaches had for Ken already-- and she gave Ken a perfect "kiss-kiss" their entire drive home. Peaches announced, "The level of certainty in our love, that I have, is beyond the restrictions of the atmosphere's limits." To which, Ken replied "The possibility of there being any limits, in an atmosphere that grants us the ability for sustaining our love, can't even exist, let alone enough to be measured!" Hearing that, Peaches heart melted, while at the same time, in nature, the world's loneliest apple tree dropped a single white apple.

CHAPTER 3

As time progressed, Ken learned that Peaches' ex had a retractable bladed knife (switchblade), which he'd pulled out on many people. There was even a claim the guy had cut someone's head off in a knife fight, but was never proven, Peaches insinuated. Ken realized that Peaches' ex-boyfriend might be dangerous, being he was obviously an unbalanced sounding individual; so, Ken bought a .357 magnum, teaching Peaches how to safely shoot it. Ken and Peaches started keeping the .357 in their nightstand drawer in case it was ever needed for protection. Life was going great!

So, Ken and Peaches arrived at the "for building" town, realizing not much change occurs with time in some places. Unfortunately, after 100 years of equality rights changes in the United States, this town's people were staring and whispering to each other at the sight of the couple that had just rolled into town--Ken and Peaches looked at each other, smiled, and thanked God they let love rule. Ken got out of the truck and walked up a sidewalk by some town's people, wanting to inquire about directions to John Lynch's old estate. After much pressing, a man pointed down the road, saying "Drive down the hill, going through the last farm field. There's a winding easement road (only pathway through someone's land to gain access to another landowner's property). You'll find the shack at the bottom." Ken thanked the fellow, hoping what the guy said wasn't a lie.

CHAPTER 4

Meanwhile, there were things occurring at the old John Lynch house. A woman known as the China Girl was upset about losing a black-gold leaf, which had been dangling from her earring but had somehow gotten lost. The China Girl and her partner had recently pulled a heist, which was done under direct orders from "The Master." The missing black-gold leaf could blow their cover, and potentially uncover the identity of "The Master," who ran the complete organization. Without the black-gold leaf, the China Girl and her partner figured it would be safer to duck-out of sight; so, they were staying (recouping) in the ramshackle remains of the old Lynch house. The China Girl worried that the leaf may have been lost at the scene of the heist location; meaning it could be finger-printed, which would be serious. The duo (China Girl and her partner) was known to others in their organization as "The Last Imperialists," and were only sent on missions of high risk--being there could be no foul-ups. China Girl's partner was a Frenchman, who looked a lot like Nicolas Cage. The Frenchman had taken an operative informant agent, who'd become a known traitor in the heist brigade mission, into custody. The Frenchman was demanding answers from the informant rat; finding out that the rat wasn't even loyal to the King, who, as it turned out, he was working for! So, the Frenchman, who looked like Nicolas Cage, took a long sword and stabbed it through the traitor's left eye, pinning the guy into the wall behind him. Before the traitor died, the Frenchman harshly asked him "Is everything alright, back at The House of France?" Before expiring, the traitor's quivering body cried a reply of "Yes, my Liege!" Once the Frenchman had his answer, he removed the sword from the traitor's skull (which had been the only thing holding the traitor's body in an upright position); causing the dead body to drop to the floor.

CHAPTER 5

Ken asked Peaches if she'd like to drive down the road, so he could start watching the fields with his binoculars; the shack was supposed to be far down a hill, with some farm field uphill from it, but Ken didn't know where exactly. Peaches found it crazy that it would've been legal to hold binoculars up & down to one's eyes and drive, even though texting and driving wasn't legal; so, she thought Ken was being very sensible to let her drive, instead of trying the binoculars and driving. Peaches knew Ken was going to be a great Father, putting it in her mind to make him one as soon as they got home. Peaches took over the wheel, driving 10-12 feet at a time, then slamming on the brakes; stopping so Ken could look around for the Lynch house. Ken found Peaches' driving skills to be cute and funny, but neither he nor Peaches saw a small Christmas tree in the roadway, which Peaches hit, causing it to get tangled up under the front bumper. The couple laughed like kids about hitting the tree, because just down the hillside from it was the ramshackle remains of the old Lynch house. Ken said "Well, Merry Christmas" and hopped out of the truck to start heaving the small tree out from under the bumper, when he noticed a black-gold leaf, marked with an odd-looking crescent, just lying there in the road. Ken knew it was real gold, so he put it in his pocket.

Before taking the truck off-roading down the farm field's hillside, Peaches made her way back to the passenger seat; allowing Ken to retake driving duties, and Ken locked the 4X4 wheel hubs (this was done manually on Ford trucks by being outside the truck, turning the front wheel hubs by hand to lock/unlock 4WD), swearing that when they get back home "We're getting a Chevy! I've had it with Ford's nonsense wheel locks!" Suddenly, Ken remembered what his dad had said once "Son, the hills are like a woman; round and curvaceous. They are easy to get lost in, so always mind which way's North and which way isn't keep your compass pointing sharp. And Son, never do them wrong!" Ken looked at Peaches and dropped a single tear. He couldn't tell her physically, but Peaches knew, saying "In the wind, he's still alive," and that's all that mattered. Ken, not having ridden the curves of the hills in a while, eagerly pulled the truck off the road, putting it into the field too quickly; causing a momentary slip of traction control, but quickly the truck regained its grip. Ken breathed deep and said "Woman," while Peaches giggled; anticipating the excitement of what off-road riding was like. Ken pressed the truck onward into the field, rolling and bouncing over the hillside bushes--the truck plowing through the almost pure virgin overgrowth of the landside. The truck's weight pounded the corners hard and fast, coming over each of the hills' curves at an outlandish pace, but that's how Ken rode them; almost dumping the load from the truck bed in the process within the first 1/3 of the way downhill. Ken was able to learn from his previous ride handling experience, keeping the cargo load from getting a mind of its own and spilling off. The ride couldn't help but start reminding Peaches of the wonderful bed that she and Ken had back at home! Slowly, they approached the shack, parking their truck snuggly against the side of the Lynch home. They noticed, after looking around some, that there were some fresh foot-trails in the tall grass, leading around the perimeter of the supposedly unoccupied old Lynch estate.

CHAPTER 6

Ken and Peaches hopped out of their truck and walked right up to the shack but were startled when the China Girl opened the front door, with the Frenchman being right behind her, glaringly looking at them through a screen door. Ken said "Hello" to the China Girl through the screen door, and then started to state what had brought him and Peaches out there. Then, through the doorway, Ken and Peaches noticed the dead body on the floor in the house; that the China Girl and Frenchman were trying their best to block from view. Ken reached behind his back, where on his left side the .357 Magnum was in a holster but was covered by an overhanging shirt. Ken nudged Peaches, letting her know exactly where the .357 was too--God forbid it turned into a "live and let die" situation. Ken wasn't trying to let on to the China Girl or Frenchman that he was armed, but the Frenchman knew; being trained as he was. The Frenchman felt it would be better to explain his and the China Girl's situation, rather than to start a fight. After all, not many people win by bringing a sword to a gunfight!

CHAPTER 7

The China Girl welcomed Ken and Peaches inside, stating "It's an odd, but explainable thing that's occurred." She started telling Ken and Peaches that she and her partner were undercover operatives who'd performed a heist from a foreign government, but that was operating on U.S. soil. Furthermore, she expressed the importance that the heist would aid the U.S. greatly. When the China Girl mentioned about losing the black-gold earring leaf, Ken started to realize this wasn't a bluff story . . . and seeing the odd crescent mark on the leaf himself, just wanting his brain to believe he'd seen what he'd seen . . . the markings on the leaf were meant for people who the U.S. Pentagon must give free reign and action, in all matters, of the entire United States. Ken, trying to explain who these people were to Peaches (Peaches not knowing Ken had the black-gold leaf in his pocket) said "Let's just say, these two could walk directly into The President of the United States' office and tell him to 'Get out! Go stand in the hall or something,' if they'd wanted to make a phone call from the President's own desk phone...even if just to hear each other's cell phone ringtone." The China Girl mentioned that if the black-gold leaf was lost at the heist scene, the odds of human existence are over for the Country anyway. Not just that, but their cover would be blown in all Countries as well. It was highly evident that this was beyond a matter of National Security, causing a reverse chill to crawl up, not down, Ken's spine. Then, the Frenchman chimed in, saying that "The dead Chap on the floor was a stinking Communist spy, double-backing with the Russians, and strong-arming French loyalists into becoming Communists under threats of persecution (on and/or out of the Country), which he could've actually made real; but that was just the "tip-of-the -iceberg!" The China Girl started saying "When it comes to the dead man, more despicable crimes against humanity have been accredited to him than those of . . . compared to any ever." Peaches, having taken a Social Studies class back in Freelance High School, understood the severity of what the China Girl and Frenchman had said, but to a broader degree than Ken did. Just then, Peaches' ex-boyfriend came rolling down the hillside embankment on an ATV. He'd followed Ken and Peaches (stalked) waiting for an opportunity to get them while they were out of the public eye and planned on ending their relationship. Ken saw the four-wheeler coming, noticing that Peaches' ex had an outstretched arm brandishing a knife (the switchblade), and that he had murder in his eyes.

Ken inquired of the Frenchman and the China Girl "If Peaches' ex-boyfriend was to just barge in here uninvited, and with a weapon pulled, he'd be trespassing on temporarily protected Government Grounds, right?" The Frenchman said "Yes." So, Ken asked "And, you would be correct, technically, to kill him for an intrusion of a caliber greater than just trespassing, correct?" The China Girl replied "Yes." Ken and Peaches looked at each other, both thinking about exiting out through the back door, when Ken pulled the black-gold leaf out from his pocket; realizing it'd been worth its weight--as well as the wait--in gold and gladly handed it over to the China Girl. Ken looked now like Optimus Prime passing on the Matrix of Leadership in the 1980's Transformers Movie and said, "Till All Are

One!" The Frenchman was elated that the China Girl got the missing black-gold leaf back, and instantly prepared himself in a defensive stance, to guard against anything coming through the front door, and repeated back to Ken "TILL ALL ARE ONE!" Ken and Peaches headed out the house's back door, not looking back, commenting to the Frenchman and China Girl "You two are the U.S.'s best kept secrets!" An echoing "Yes" was declared by both the Frenchman and the China Girl, and the house's back door shut tightly. At the same moment Peaches' ex came storming into the old Lynch house through the front door, uninvited, and swinging his knife. *THUD* was the only sound heard.

Ken and Peaches climbed into their truck, turned and smiled at each other, then headed for home. "Thank You, Forever, John Lynch" was worded into both of their wedding vows later that summer . . . that and some water faucet references.

-The End-

THE LEGENDARY'S

This is the story of three of baseball's greatest fictional players. They are known only by their nicknames. Fans would find it hard to believe these players weren't born by the given personages. The impact of these greats on the game was something like Walt Disney animating a Playboy magazine while listening to a Roy Orbison tune--anything you want. These are The Legendary's!

LEGEND #1

K-Mart: A 1940's slugger who never hit the stadium lighting itself, but graced home-run balls out of the ballpark by millimeters edge of the grandstand lights. The solar eclipse is a good example for reference here. When the corona of the sun is visible as the moon (moon acting as the baseball) passes by, the edge of light shows a blue colored hue to those watching. K-Mart made it a point to knock balls out of the ballpark in night games, edging past the lighting, which gave a bluish tinge of luminescence. He called his wild homers the "blue light special" and everyone called him K-Mart for them.

LEGEND #2

The Iceman: This rare jewel was the product of the modern refrigeration evolution. The Iceman started out using freezing therapy on his thumbs, limbs, and his back. Cryotherapy is for injured people, but the Iceman wasn't injured (yet). After getting his entire body used to the treatments, he became accustomed to sitting in the walk-in-cooler (like liquor stores have) at the ballpark. When his team required their heavy hitter, he would literally walk up to the plate directly from the cooler. Cold steam rising about from this figure at the diamond penetrated fear into every pitcher he faced.

Some guitar players don't believe in warming up before playing; they feel it wrecks the purity of their performance to warm up first. The Iceman believed in the art of cold play, taking it to what some might say is extreme. It might be lucky, but it worked! Though he only played professionally for two seasons before needing to use a hot pad (Doctors orders); for his back, ending his baseball career, he left the game as one of the hottest coldest players ever.

LEGEND #3

Walk Don't Run: Whoa Mama, this guy intimated everyone in his presence. It is claimed, in his youth, Walk Don't Run was hit in the forehead by the very first pitch he ever faced. It is also claimed that he proceeded to hit the ball using his forehead. Either way, he glared at the opposing team as he gradually took his "hit by pitch" base. Approaching the base (as if nothing happened), it's said he did not stop at first; Walk Don't Run, squinting and staring at everyone on field, continuing, took second base too! W.D.R. made it seem as if they owed him more, setting a new precedence that no one has followed since. History records go silent for the rest of Walk Don't Run during his youth years; we next hear of him in the majors.

Every, and I mean every league team manager told their pitcher to "Walk that guy!" One day, a young rookie disobeyed: big mistake! While trying to make a name for himself, the now homeless pitcher decided to throw W.D.R. a "screwball." W.D.R. saw it coming from a mile away, while cracking a half smile, and making a hmphed sound in interest. The growly sound was audible to everyone, even over the gasps of the crowd. With the baseball coming in hot, W.D.R. gestured (holding the whole time) the middle finger of his left hand to the young pitcher. With his right hand he pointed to the bat's indented head--as if to poke the ball--like a pool cue. With aim true as can be, W.D.R. speared the baseball! Before the ball could even deflect from the bat, he impaled the ball 4" into the ground, leaving the bat sticking up from the earth above it. The ball never crossed home plate; it was shy by over an inch. With the bat protruding from the fields' turf, it stood like King

Arthur's sword (the Excalibur). No one on the field (infield or outfield) came to attempt pulling the bat from the earth. Walk Don't Run walked all the bases nonchalantly that day.

In the case of the baseball's corpse, I heard every word that was said (I was a young reporter attending the game when it occurred). Directly quoting the entire opposing team (unanimously)-- minus the pitcher--they asked the umpire to "Just bury the ball, along with that pitcher's career!"

FINAL #4

Well, that's the story of The Legendary's. You may be wondering why Telephone to China and his "long distance call," or Freight Train and the "direct express" didn't make the list. Simple answer...they'd both delivered so fast (early), before anyone saw or knew they were even there, that subsequently time got lost in the shuffle.

-The End

KENNETH KRUSCHKA

ONE OF THOSE DAYS

PART 1

I was one of those days that everyone experiences at some point in life, where nothing seems to go as expected; slowly progressing downward from how the day started. Perry was having just such a day, which has been recorded here.

Perry had almost gotten through another workweek and wasn't going to miss a chance at getting a date with his new, blonde, female co-worker (whom all the guys were drooling after), before making any other plans with his T.G.I.F. night. Perry walked up to her and asked, "Do you like those hamburgers at Joe's?"--he could only think up the old "Eat at Joe's" expression, so tried to incorporate it in a clever way; bombing in the process. The blonde woman coughed (exaggeratedly) at his question, as if he'd rudely interrupted her in the middle of an important conversation (she was alone and filing her nails, counting down the last 5 minutes of the day, before getting off work), and harshly replied "I don't eat there!" before turning her head away from Perry altogether. Perry had tried talking about food, hoping to make her hungry, but it was a classic case of "everything on the left should've been on the right:" Way incompatible. Perry left work feeling dejected and decided to go home, before making plans on how to spend his evening.

PART 2

On the drive home from work, Perry got stuck in grid-lock traffic; wasting a lot of time, attempting to slowly front his way through it. Finally, once arriving home, he made a command decision to take a shower before changing to go out on the town for the evening. While showering, an angry wasp flew into the shower stall, leaving Perry half clean, naked, wet, and jumping out of the bathtub--his shower was over. The ordeal left Perry feeling very unclean, and not wanting to be around people, in public, that way. He started toiling with different ideas about how to spend the night at home, instead of going out.

Perry threw on some clothes, going with a sweats, t-shirt, and sneakers look (dressing for comfort vs. style), before heading downstairs from the shower fiasco. Then, he let his dog out to go potty, as was the normal routine. When the dog started coming back in from "doing the deed," it bolted (ran like hell) back into the apartment, almost knocking Perry down in the process. Perry had barely shut the door, noticing through the door's window that a grey colored, adult, lynx was walking--one might even say it was hunting-- alongside the building. This, for certain, deterred him from wanting to go out anywhere that night. As if the coyotes in the area, which were big as good-sized dogs, weren't bad enough, now there was a lynx to be alert for.

Starting to get hungry, Perry headed over to his refrigerator's freezer, finding about $25.00 worth of different flavors of ice cream, which he owed to the maintenance guy for fixing a roof leak recently. Since that individual wasn't present, and he wasn't about to wrestle with the animal outside his door-- let alone in the dark--he declared "Ice cream for dinner and watching TV is how I'll spend this glorious evening!" He was relieved that a plan was finally set, being his options were getting kind of thin.

PART 3

The dog watched eagerly as Perry dished himself up a giant bowl of ice cream, which was heaped beyond the bowl's top, consisting of many different scoops (enough to be considered a meal, not just a snack) from the array of flavors he'd had on hand. The dog started drooling, opening his eyes wide, and focused all its attention on finding an opportunity to sneak a taste of ice cream; waiting, knowing better than to get caught doing it. Perry, setting his dish of ice cream on a coffee table and walking across the living room, going to retrieve the TV's remote from his entertainment center, was when the dog saw its perfect time. The dog (unnoticed) was able to devour an entire scoop worth of cherry flavored ice cream; making it disappear in a Guinness-records-breaking 2-seconds flat.

Perry returned with the TV remote, picked up his dish of ice cream, and kicked back onto the sofa couch behind the coffee table, thinking out loud "Humm . . . this dish is lighter than I remember." Turning on the TV, not thinking much about it again, Perry started eating, but noticed how oddly the top ice cream seemed to have melted already. Not exactly sure what time it was, he deduced it must be after 10 P.M., because the weekly updates were on all the free TV channels: --" . . . Santa's sleigh has something on its way!" -- "The transgender of Wembley . . ." - -"A military bus was turned into an Italian restaurant, but immigrants . . . "--" . . . how a (*expletive*) propane torch should work is . . ." No! No! No! Perry cried. After skipping through all the channels, it became painfully apparent that nothing good was on, so he chose to watch cable television instead. Perry knew there were some infomercials on during the night, so he made it a point to scout them out;

figuring that, worst case, he'd fall asleep watching one and wind up dreaming about it. Suddenly, he recalled a book he'd read, a long, long, time ago, where an old (500 years in age) phoenix bird was always giving advice to a boy, David, like: "We shall sleep during the day and continue your education at night!" and "Knowledge is power!"

"That's it!" Perry cheered, deciding to learn whatever he could from any infomercials he'd end up watching. Perry brought his notepad paper and a pencil up from under the coffee table; opting to take notes, should some infomercial cause him to. Almost as if the TV had waited for Perry to be looking, an Arabian guy holding a white bird came on the screen, not saying anything till Perry looked at him! The guy was claiming that: "Simply by joining in a 5- or 6-year contract commitment, you can improve your credit score," to which the bird started parroting "credit score, credit score." Perry grabbed his pencil and paper, jotting in big letters: DECLINE! The next sales-pitch started as soon as he put the paper aside. It had a group of paramedics (actor portrayals) who weren't speaking loud enough to hear, so Perry turned the volume up to maximum level, which, of course, is when the sound of their ambulance siren blared loud & clear through the TV speakers-- silence is truly golden after all. Perry never did figure out what they were attempting to sell and wondered if his ears might be bleeding. Disgusted with his TV experience thus far, Perry looked out his front window, which faced the neighbor across the street's bathroom window. He noticed that the lady over there was topless and in full view, but once catching a glimpse of her, she turned down her lights for the night. "Isn't that lucky!" Perry dramatically huffed, while shaking his head and checking the time; realizing it was almost midnight. He decided that he, too, would turn off his room lights; believing that the TV experience could, somehow, be enhanced by watching in the dark, and explained to his dog--like he had some ancient, secret, Chinese answer--"This works for the movie theaters, even if they're playing a bad film."

PART 4

Returning to his couch seat, after turning off the room lights, Perry really nestled himself into his seat. He'd hoped the after-midnight programming might be a more promising watch. The first load of malarkey was already playing, which involved a device like a washing machine, but washed clothing while it was hung in one's closet. "What an idea!" Perry shouted, while at the same time gasping at the thought. Quickly making a note on his sheet of paper, he wrote "Can't wait till they install floating bathtubs." Then, the next gimmick started on the TV channel (one right into the next). Perry realized there were NO commercial breaks in between, what were, in-and-of-themselves, truly, just commercials themselves, and said: "Why, those dogs!" which, oddly, turned out to be exactly what they were selling in the infomercial. There were 4 dogs, all of which were flying miniature stunt planes, each bearing the markings of a different country across the wings. The dogs all had different names too. Perry watched as the pilot dog, named Spaghetti, was (supposedly) trying to find America, but was unaware it was already there. The entire 1/64th scale miniatures set, made of die-cast metal, was being sold as "limited time keepsake souvenirs," and running a 1-800 number across the screen bottom, while a Garth Brooks song played--which had nothing to do with dogs or planes. Perry scolded the TV: "I'll bet my coat! It's only a matter of time before the 'keepsake souvenirs' wind-up donated, by the dozens, at Goodwill stores."

Perry exclaimed "OH, this is terrible!" and violently shut off the TV, in a manner reminiscent of slamming a telephone to hang-up on telemarketers. He'd made up his mind, opting instead to listen to some radio. As he walked across the room to turn the radio on, he reaffirmed himself in the belief of: "If you can't do something on your own, it isn't worth doing." Flipping on the stereo, which was on FM, an old audio recording was on, of a gentleman speaking as fireside music softly played. The man was stressing the importance of "Saying what you want, when you want!" to which Perry agreed and remarked "What truer motivational words could be spoken."

Deciding to switch the radio to AM--which is almost a lost art--Perry started the process of fine-tuning into 1087, which was the sports station. The radio, being an older unit, required tuning between frequency indicator markings in a "just so" way. The process was such: First turning the dial just a little to the left of area of the station; then, back a little to the right of frequency indicator line; then, back to the left a smidge-- or the station would come in with lots of static, which is very annoying to listen to (sometimes, even cross-receiving 2 frequencies at the same time; which is the absolute pits of a way to listen to any sports game). Perry asked himself, exclaiming his frustrations into the general air: "Is everybody's radio this finicky?!" Then, like magic, the sportscaster came through clearly, saying "At the convention hall, those professional cake-testers set a new world's record tasting cakes," then continued with an attempt at a joke "Would've been nice if they'd had some ice cream too. Get it . . . cake and ice cream!" The sportscaster was no comedian, although Perry was glad to hear that his dinner was the missing link in someone's day's event. The person speaking changed to a female, talking about the new draft-pick rookie, who'd just had their first major-league moment. She said: "New Brewers player puts on jersey, believing it said number 05, but doesn't see it said number 50 till wearing it out on the field." Perry whimpered "OH, for Christ's sakes" then blindly (unaware of his loudness) proclaimed "They're not winning this season!"

In an act of random despair, Perry, not looking, flung the radio's dial to wherever . . . an act that would've left William S. Burroughs stunned; providing an answer to the question of "How random is random?" Suddenly, a lady's voice was coming through the stereo speakers, talking about flat, decorative, wall-hangings. She was selling Christmas tree shaped hangings, both in black and white, as well as some that lit up without the use of electricity. A man who'd invested in her products chimed in, saying "They're made from rolling and gluing 2 types of fabric together . . . and it isn't even flammable." Perry considered buying one of the fine decorations, which was when he knew for sure it was bedtime and turned off the radio.

PART 5

As Perry started heading to his bedroom, he noticed his coat hanging on the staircase banister. Pausing for a moment, he decided to stop and check its pockets (hoping there might be some money in them) as a last-ditch effort for any fun that night. All that he found in the pockets--which he'd thoroughly checked, as if it was his purpose in life--was 1 lousy cough-drop, so he attempted to guess it's expiration date; finding it to be 3 or 4 years past (the label was worn down from rubbing in the pocket, making the number unreadable) the freshness date. "That's it!" Perry growled, not caring about it and decided to eat the thing anyway. After all his efforts, he was now intent on dreaming about inventing and selling floating bathtubs and declining to pitch his idea to anyone.

The End

◆ ◆ ◆

DEVIN

PART 1

D evin was without a vehicle, for the umpteenth time--which was nothing new, being he didn't have transportation more often than he did--because he'd overdone it at a drinking party (blaming its host, Adam, as the reason he'd drank too much), so had conned his now ex-girlfriend, Kim, to drive instead. Kim, being just as drunk as Devin, and unfamiliar with the vehicle (from the driver's perspective but knew the backseat well) got the vehicle (an SUV) into an accident; by backing it right into a trailer, which was parked in Adam's driveway. Devin had borrowed the SUV from his mom, so with the vehicle now having: a smashed right-side taillight, dented rear hatch, and some minor paint damage, his mom wasn't about to lend him the SUV again--least not anytime soon. So, without his own transportation, Devin had been walking everywhere, or bumming rides from friends--not to mention bumming: cigarettes, money, and flat-out stealing from people, which his friends were trying their best not to notice.

One day, as Devin was footing his way over to Donny's place, he got an idea for a song. As it was, he'd happened to have borrowed a Dictaphone from a friend, Ben, and had it in his jacket pocket; so, pulled it out and decided he mind-as-well recorded what was going through his head. Devin really had meant to return the Dictaphone, though he'd been borrowing it for so long that most people would've given up hope of ever receiving back their loaned-out item; so, he didn't feel the need to rush. Devin figured that if he continued, at a walking pace, he would have about 10 minutes before getting to Donny's house. Pressing the record on the Dictaphone, Devin started singing "On a baseball field, it isn't the base, it's where you begin! It's all in a secret place, in a secret world." Devin stopped recording, wondering if a Fender guitar riff should accompany his lyrics. He'd made it over to Donny's house, which was located on Easy Street--it's true, seemingly no one works over on Easy Street. Devin had always believed that Donny had "the life," even though there was nothing to support that thought! Donny was the kind of guy who'd rather get drunk and go sleep in a closet at a friend's house, rather than to go home and face his old lady. Donny was almost pushed into putting two houses together, but he couldn't even stand the one he had.

Devin went to press the doorbell when, suddenly, Donny quickly opened the inside door, wearing only his boxer shorts. Donny wasn't surprised that Devin came over, though he found it awfully rude Devin didn't call first; choosing instead to stop over unannounced. Donny just wanted to "smoke a bowl," so pulled a big hit off his glass pipe, which turned out to be more a resin hit than an actual bud. Donny opened the screen door, exhaled a huge cloud of smoke into Devin's face, and then continually coughed while asking Devin "What up?" Devin took the pipe from Donny, looking to get stoned himself, but noticed the bowl was empty (ash beyond cash) and gave Donny a W.T.F. look. Devin went over to a crack in Donny's porch step, which was where he'd been stashing his weed, pulling a baggie with a 1/8th oz. of Jamaican Red, laced with acid, out from the not-so-secret hiding spot. Devin packed a bowl, which glowed bright orange once his lighter's flame bent down into the pipe; setting seeds popping and some stems burning like wood, while he inhaled deeply. Devin coughed, then cursed his supplier "What's this, shake! Damn seeds 'n stems!" Picking out the thing he should've before lighting up (mainly, the stem, it was too late for the seeds), Devin took another hit while the bowl was still lit; being quick enough to not need relighting, which was cool. Being a big believer in "puff-puff-pass," Devin was just about to pass the pipe over to Donny when he spotted some undercover officers pulling up and parking on the street.

Quickly, Devin tossed the glass pipe, ditching it into the bushes down the side of the property. Donny proclaimed, "Their heading to whoever's in that house is going to get fucked!" Devin knew Donny was way baked (really stoned), so whatever he'd said, and had meant to say, juxtaposed together, but it made sense enough. Devin replied, "Just as long as it isn't here!" Donny was upset that Devin threw his ganja pipe, so he made him retrieve it. Devin found out that retrieving the pipe was easier said than done, picking up a dead mouse from under a bush by mistake. After finding the pipe (luckily unbroken) and repacking the bowl, Devin and Donny toked up till they decided they had had enough. While he Chief'd up, Devin was considering what he should do after he leaves Donny's place, being he had nowhere in particular to be--being unemployed, in part, was because he didn't have a vehicle to get to/from a job, so he wasted his days getting high and doing nothing. Then, it dawned on Devin, his friend, Ben, had some professional audio recording equipment set-up in his basement. Devin thought, maybe, he could get his song transferred from the Dictaphone over to a tape . . . though, if he wasn't so analog minded, a CD would've made more sense. Devin left Donny's, acting unsuspicious as he walked past the undercover officers, and started heading to Ben's house.

PART 2

Ben had been seeing two girls at the same time; neither of the girls knew about the other (at least Ben believed). Recently, an extra pair of shoes was left sitting in the enclosed front porch of Ben's house, assumed to be from one-or-the-other of his lady friends, and causing suspicion to the one whose shoes they weren't. Ben had noticed them sitting but didn't want to ask the wrong lady friend about them either. The shoes had become "the silent elephant in the room," but Ben worried they might be from someone (a third lady) else altogether. Ben thought about his ex-girlfriend, Kelly, who would spy on him in many ways: hiding her car around corners; watching, waiting to follow if he left; acting like she was driving away, leaving then sneaking back in the house. CRAZY! Ben wondered how the odds were of Kelly planting the shoes, trying to start some drama with him and his lady friends . . . and if so, could he find time to squeeze her back in as a third girlfriend? Ben didn't know, but reflected on how the sex was with Kelly, deeming it incredible (unlike with his two current lady friends). Then, he remembered a time when he'd had Kelly downstairs and a new lady friend upstairs, unbeknownst to either of the women! Ben decided two girlfriends were enough, shaking off his silly thought about room for another. Devin had helped conduct Ben's "traffic," keeping him from getting caught on several occasions, which Ben appreciated about Devin's friendship.

Devin made it over to Ben's house, unannounced, and rapped out the old "Shave and a haircut, two bits" on the door's knocking device. A stomping rush (which could be felt shaking the house, from on the front porch) came thudding towards answering the front door, which was Ben's 300+ pound lady friend, Rachel. Rachel was upset, huffing about being pulled away from her Harry Potter movie, so she stomped all the way over to the door. Rachel barely opened the door any (maybe an inch), not greeting who was at the door, then just turned around and headed back to her living room seat, picking up watching her movie. Devin, standing, facing the pretty much still closed door, realized he'd been expected to let himself in, exclaimed "How asinine!" After coming in the house, he made it a point to shut the front door loudly--slammed the darn thing but won't admit it--enough so that it would disturb Rachel's movie watching. Devin deliberately used an interrobang on Rachel, inquiring and scolding her with the same sentence, stating "That's your first time answering a door?!" Ben, hearing Devin upstairs, called him to come down to the basement.

Eventually, Devin made his way through the house (it's believed that he stopped to flip Rachel off, for somewhere around two minutes, completely unnoticed, as he passed her in the living room) and down the split rear staircase, leading to the basement. As Devin was coming down the last couple stairs, he saw Ben painting a giant sun with a face; looking much like the one on the back of The Smashing Pumpkins "Mellon Collie and the Infinite Sadness" album; however, Ben's sun was blowing fire down at the star constellations. There was a plastic wrapped plate of food on the table by Ben, so Devin headed straight to it and started to open the saran wrap covering plate. Ben caught him and warned him "If you eat it, you have to serve 4 others at the Jesus place!" continuing that "It's a way Rachel's trying to tie me down, so she can keep her bulging eyes on me. I'm playing the game right back...She's going to lose and can eat it herself!" Really, it just proved there was a war going on between the couple. Devin had witnessed some of the "games" that Ben and Rachel played with each other: Rachel jumping on Ben's back, pulling his arms behind him like reins on a horse, and then riding him around like a pony. Ben had a silent word game (after witnessing it enough, it became evident it was a silent word game) where if Rachel said a certain thing (word of the day?) he'd grab her bare foot and smack its bottom hard--like spanking a baby or something. A slap like that would surely leave one's hand stinging, so Devin assumed it was a kinky, bare-foot fetish thing.

PART 3

D evin was in the process of preparing his nerves, wanting to ask Ben about the audio recording equipment to record his song from the Dictaphone, when he noticed 6 boxes full of VHS tapes; 5 of the boxes being labeled "Friends, the complete seasons." There it was, every single episode of the hit TV show, Friends, all scattered about into 40lbs worth of VHS tapes (not exact weight, but close), creating the complete series 10 seasons. Devin knew his mom loved that show, and DVD prices for such a long series aren't cheap--Devin's into saving money--so, he pondered a thought of some way to swindle Ben out of the VHS tapes.

Finally, Devin asked Ben if he could use the recording equipment to copy his song from the Dictaphone, before giving it back. Ben answered him, "I think we can work something out." He'd noticed Devin was eyeing up the VHS tape boxes with interest, which Rachel had moved into the house without telling Ben. It was apparent to Ben that Rachel had started nesting, so he was fine with moving out anything she'd moved in. Out of nowhere, Ben commented to Devin that "You know, for a bigger girl, Rachel's got a jokingly small butt!" Devin chuckled at the observation, and then insinuated "Some chicks are into that." Ben brought over a DVD in a CD's case, containing a video he'd been cropping together; it just needed some audio duped in yet for a music soundtrack. The music Ben had been tinkering with wasn't working with the scenery; it was mostly high-school marching bands, so he'd shelved the project till something better came along. Devin's singing, on the other hand, was better for splicing in with the video; but his song was a bit too short, so he'd need to record a few more lyrics. Quickly hitting the record button, Devin started chanting "Coming at man from bending sheep, YA, it's the exact words for a Pyre's death! Don't you know all the people of the king?" Although the lyrics had nothing to do with the previous ones, for the application they'd be used in they were fine. Devin cheered "That's tight!"

PART 4

Now that the recording was done, Ben and Devin sat down for a celebratory cigarette and 6-pack of Coors light, toasting cheers to the new song. Ben was highly aware that Devin had a tin ear, so was really toasting (silently) to Devin stopping singing. Ben started drawing a picture of an Irish leprechaun wearing 2 pairs of sunglasses; one set covering a second pair of eyes that creepily looked out through the leprechaun's top hat and drew it holding a dope pipe. Before long, Devin had opened one of the VHS tapes filled boxes, wanting to test play a tape to see if they'd even work. Ben and Devin put the tape in a VCR and watched a show called Underwater Wall Repair Work, which was on a tape that also had an episode of Friends on it. The show they watched, though, pertained to the repair of load-bearing walls in waters where sharks are present. A worker (this guy certainly wasn't an actor) on the show claimed "The best one can hope for, if a shark gets hold of you, is that a friend (meaning co-worker, friend, passing observer, anybody) shoots the shark that's killing you. Only a fast-repeating gun will do in that situation, that's why we keep this (holds up an AR-15) gun in our jobsite toolbox." It was painfully evident the tape was recorded from TV in the '90's. Ben stopped the tape and tried to hustle Devin a little, saying "Yep, somewhere collectively on all these tapes are every single episode of the classic Friends TV show, and if you want to use my audio equipment any further you must agree to take all these VHS tapes with you-- for free mind you--when you leave. Rachel won't sneak things into this basement again without me knowing, so let it be a lesson to her!" Devin cringed and accepted the offer. Then, Ben upped the ante, betting Devin $5.00 that he couldn't con Rachel into giving him a ride back to his mom's house; because she'd have to haul all the VHS tapes with her, being a stipulation of the audio equipment use agreement to Devin's needing to take all the tapes with when he leaves. Devin boldly accepted Ben's (calling him a bastard, over and over) terms of the bet.

With a Hawaiian ocean-like body of water in the background, and multi-square, multi-colored disco floor, outside in the forefront, Elvis Presley and John Lennon take the stage (dance floor) together. Ben thought, being a Photoshopped piece of video that Devin was laying his music track over with, was an impressive feat of audio dubbing. Ben suggested that the screen should flash, in big 3D letters, something like "Do the Elliptical Tomorrow;" giving the song its own counterpart dance name and giving John Lennon and Elvis Presley a Disco song; neither was ever known for being Disco music artists. What Devin was doing made it seem like Elvis and John had collaborated and created a '70's dance craze. Anyway, Elvis and John Lennon are supposedly in 1977, with Elvis wearing a fake mustache and looking very intently at the film camera, over the top of his dark, copper-colored sunglasses. As the tape continues playing, Elvis prances directly across the dance floor and

John Lennon runs across it (was it a race?), just for the sport of getting on the Disco floor--Elvis really didn't stand a chance in Hell of winning if it was a race. Devin thought out loud "Sure makes an interesting film, even if it's doctored." Devin was devising his plan to win the bet he'd taken with Ben, being he'd started sobering up by this time and had realized his song blew; though he knew how to put it to use, in total with the video, now. Devin knew Rachel liked Elvis, as she'd had an Elvis bumper sticker on her vehicle, and he needed to craft his scam well (getting Rachel to succumb to its crookedness, not pull away). So, as a cherry on the top, Devin drew up a cartoon depiction of Elvis smoking a cigarette as the front cover sleeve art to the CD case, which was what the DVD of the Photoshopped music-video of his song was placed in.

PART 5

Devin knew putting all the VHS tape boxes outside wasn't going to work without Rachel's noticing . . . all the trips carrying them to his mom's place didn't sound fun either. Studying what was at his disposal around the basement, that might be worthy of transporting the VHS tape boxes, there was: a Marshall amplifier for guitar, a toolbox--already full and in use, and a standing dresser. The dresser was 5 drawers tall and was completely empty, so it was perfect. Devin asked Ben if he could borrow the dresser, to which Ben agreed, raising an eyebrow in curiosity. Devin packed the 5 boxes of tapes marked Friends into the dresser, 1 box to each of the 5 drawers, then thought about what to do with the 6th; being it was not marked Friends, so not part of the series collection. It was just a useless annoyance to his plan. Devin put the 6th box of VHS tapes into a heavy-duty 30-gallon trash bag, planning to walk it right outside, acting like he was just doing Ben a favor by taking out the basement's trash can bag. Devin planned to walk the full garbage bag down the block, where there was an apartment's dumpster, and then pitch it. He remembered it was really muddy down by those apartments, so he took the extra pair of shoes from on the front porch, with him on his way out; planning to change into them when walking through the muddy area surrounding the dumpster, then just leaving them down there and switching back into his regular shoes after getting out of the mud (keeping his shoes clean in the process). The plan worked and Devin returned to Ben's house one bag lighter, acting like he'd just gone out for a cigarette (incase Rachel was watching), which made him want a cigarette, so getting back in the basement he stole a Maverick menthol from Ben's pack and lit it. Rachel was clueless! Devin then asked Ben to go upstairs and deliver the customized DVD to Rachel, who was still a lump, watching TV. Devin told Ben he needed his help to move the dresser, so to "Come back down immediately after you give her that steaming heap (referring to the DVD)." Ben went upstairs, delivered Rachel the DVD, quickly grabbed a beer from the fridge, and then headed back down to the basement.

Rachel, seeing the Elvis cartoon image, jumped from her seat--she had been sprawled out, hogging the entirety of the couch--eager to insert the disc into the DVD player. Devin could hear every one of Rachel's steps, thumping their way across the living room to and from the DVD player; noticing it sounded like she was in a rush to get it in and playing. Devin knew he needed to time things "just so," so that Rachel would have enough time to build up an opinion of the gesture of receiving the present. While the DVD played, Devin and Ben loaded the dresser, containing the 5 full boxes of VHS tapes, into Rachel's minivan. Devin made the sign of the cross, knowing that from here forward things were based only on luck.

PART 6

Rachel was watching the customized video, thinking that Devin had made it just for her (being naive and arrogant), and quietly said "HE probably made it as a way to apologize to me. How sweet!" That's when Ben and Devin chanced to walk into the living room, waiting till Rachel was all "warm & fuzzy" feeling from seeing some Elvis. They were talking about the dresser, Devin mentioning how grateful he was that Ben had the minivan in the driveway to move it, and asked "How much did such an exquisite vehicle cost these days?" Rachel chimed in "That's my minivan. What happened?" Devin, knowing it was hers all along, had to play it cool and said "Oh, oops! I thought it was Ben's van. I've put a dresser that Ben lent me in the van's cargo area, if Ben would let me use the van to get it home. Rachel couldn't help but feel bad; being the guy must've been so down on his luck, needing to borrow an old dresser. She'd surprised herself to realize she even cared at all (thanks to the video gift, her feelings were tweaked) and said "Ben isn't insured to drive my van, so he couldn't drive it anywhere . . . why, it's illegal to drive without insurance in this state. You're staying at your mother's house, correct? Well, that's just a few minutes away, so why don't I just run you over there quickly. I really am glad to be able to help the needy." The last part of her answer was going a bit too far (as she often did); getting on her "high horse" again, but Devin needed the ride from her, if he was to succeed with his plan; so, he chose to bite his tongue, rather than say something. Inside himself, Devin was shouting "Damn, I'm good!"

After Rachel scurried around, not saying what she was looking for, she said "Ok, let's go," but was wearing a pair of slippers that looked like Ben's. Devin didn't say he'd taken her shoes, and Ben had no clue about it either, so the shoe mystery had just gotten a little bit weirder. The next 15 minutes riding in the minivan with Rachel were intense. Devin felt every bump and turn as a matter of life or death; the dresser making mysterious load-shifting noises. Luckily, Rachel never noticed, or at least thought nothing of it, with her power to ignore the most important things. Devin felt something in his jacket pocket, pulling out a $5.00 bill with a paperclip holding a note to it. Rachel looked over, but Devin didn't read it to her. The note said "If you're reading this and haven't gotten caught, you've just won the bet, so here's your $5.00. P.S. You're one heck of a hustler!" Devin put 2+2 together, realizing that Ben must've put the note in his pocket while they were talking in the living room.

Devin and Rachel arrived at Devin's Mom's house, so Devin jumped out of the minivan saying, "I got this," as he walked to the tailgate, opened it, then pushed the dresser out of the van. The dresser fell to the ground, lying flat on its back. Rachel's jaw dropped, thinking "He must be out of his frozen, fucking mind!" He was trying not to allude to the fact that the dresser was full of weight, so he didn't want to chance standing the thing upright till after Rachel left. Rachel, seeing how violent the dresser fell, wasn't inclined to getting her toes squashed, let alone in slippers, helping him move the thing anyway. Devin looked at Rachel, then said "I'll . . . I'll deal with it later. Hey, thanks for the lift." Meanwhile, Ben had called his other lady friend, taking advantage of Rachel's absence. He was inquiring about her, what time he might expect her to slide by that night.

As soon as Rachel had driven out of sight, Devin yelled for his mom to come outside. "Mom, come see the gift I got for you!" He shouted over and over, but it only took her a minute to come to him. Devin opened a drawer, showing his mother all the VHS tapes, and explained that they had every episode of her favorite TV show (Friends) on them.

Devin said "Mom, I won a bet to get you these!" Her reaction was priceless. She was ecstatic about receiving such a gift; causing her to come right out offering Devin full use of driving her SUV again. For the rest of the evening, she made trips from the dresser to the house, unloading a handful of the VHS tapes at a time.

Devin didn't hang around home too long. He grabbed the SUV's keys, and then quickly called Ben from the house's phone. Devin told Ben "I'm driving again," to which Ben replied, "I still haven't eaten yet!" Devin hung up the phone, jumped in the SUV, and got back on the road again.

-The End-

THE KANKAKEE
TRAIL GHOSTS

CHAPTER 1

There's a small town in Northern Wisconsin, where all the old regulations are still in common use; nothing seems to change, and people there don't question many things. As a community, the local people come together at weekends to play the hand bells, and to reflect over the town's historic Civil War era cannon. This small town has one lingering issue though, which has been wreaking havoc in recent times: leaving the locals feeling helpless.

Thor and his friend Barney were driving to the town, following specific directions a friend of Barney's had sent; along with a newspaper clipping regarding the Kankakee Nature Trail, and the possibility of its being haunted. When Barney tried to get in touch with his friend though, a mutual acquaintance of theirs told him "I'm sorry Barney! Cowboy hasn't been seen in three years. It was almost as if he'd just disappeared; leaving all his possessions behind." Barney remembered his missing comrade better once the mutual acquaintance referred to him as Cowboy--the guy had always worn a cowboy hat, no matter the season or time of day.

CHAPTER 2

As the roads started changing from urban to rural, the farther north (away from the city) Thor and Barney drove, the two started complaining about how poorly the railroad tracks were designed in the country. They'd noticed there were no alarms, bells, lights, or anything like there is in the city; just tracks. Thor commented "Up north, you just got to know when to stop for them!" Barney couldn't stop holding onto their truck's dashboard; as if bracing for impact, should a train hit them--not that it would do any good if that occurred. They'd gotten quite scared when, at an intersection, they'd stopped the truck; unable to see clearly around a corner, where a cornfield was blocking the field of vision. With Thor behind the wheel, and an engulfed view all around, neither Thor nor Barney could see a thing in any direction. Thor slowly crept the truck forward, inching it onto a train track, which was in the middle of an unmarked railroad crossing at the intersection. Once Thor could, finally, get a clear view down the tracks, he and Barney were presented with an oncoming steam engine locomotive, which required the need to floor the truck's accelerator to avoid being hit by the oncoming train. Out of nowhere, cop lights immediately started flashing. The local sheriff put it like this: "I was writing them a warning ticket for speeding, and Mr. Thor said 'I needed to pull over after that race with the rusty iron rail from Petticoat Junction! My buddy, Barney, and I found ourselves jumping out of the truck, as soon as we got to the other side of that (points at the intersection) deathtrap, and kissing the ground, clouds in the sky, and who or what ever!' so, being I'd actually seen it all happen, I was just giving them a warning ticket as a way to welcome them to the community."

CHAPTER 3

Barney took over driving, letting Thor play passenger, after the train and sheriff incident. The truck wasn't anything fancy; just an open bedded pickup, painted black. Barney wanted Thor to get some rest before they arrived at the Kankakee Nature Trail, to be alert for any ghost activity they might encounter. Thor, watching the outside scenery passing by from the passenger side window, noticed how some things stood out which could only be seen in the country: dilapidated barns; farm after farm after farm; and someone burning garbage with newspapers in a 50-gallon steel barrel, right in their front yard. Thor remarked "We're definitely in Hicksville!" Thor noticed how every wooden telephone pole in the area was bent (warped due to years of service and weather beatings), and most of the transformers, up at the pole tops, were 40 years antiquated. Thor, just about ready to take a nap, saw a guy sitting in an outhouse; with his pants around his ankles, no door, and waving hello at them as they passed by. Thor, realizing what he'd just seen said "Ouch, my eyes!" Barney chimed in, saying "We need fuel," so he pulled the truck over into a driveway where there were lots of automobiles scattered about the yard. Some of the vehicles in the yard looked like '30's and '40's gangster cars, judging by appearance (old bullet holes), but most of the cars--if not all--were well beyond any & all restoration effort.

It wasn't a minute after Thor and Barney pulled into the driveway, that a one-handed black man came out to greet them. The man was suspicious of Thor and Barney, but politely asked "Can I give you two fellas a hand?" Barney stated their need for fuel for the truck. Suddenly, a Caucasian girl appeared, frolicking around one of the junk cars before coming over by the black man's side. She'd been chasing two $5 dollar bills, which the wind had been blowing around, and she'd finally caught them; so was bringing them over to the one-handed guy to split the "findings." The one-handed fella told Barney that he'd sell him 10 gallons of fuel, which were being set aside for the upcoming winter. The black man then proceeded to fill the truck from two 5-gallon gas cans; each made of metal with a wooden handle, and each having the word GASOLENE in big, yellow lettering, angled across the front of each can. Thor figured the age of the cans to be 60 years old; judging by comparisons of ones he'd seen in antiques stores. The one-handed guy told Thor and Barney "I found a whole lotta money down there (pointing up the road) in a garbage filled storm drain." Barney said "Really?!" He wasn't sure if the guy was pulling his leg, or if he was potentially going to rob him. Barney paid the man for filling up the truck with fuel, to which the man said, "Have a nice day fella!" Thor and Barney pulled out of the driveway, starting their way up the road, when a car driving like a ballistic missile came at them head on. Barney pressed on but in a-blink-of-an-eye decided to continue using the road's shoulder lane; to be over as far as possible from the crazy oncoming vehicle. As the car passed Barney and Thor, they thought it was a Cadillac Eldorado from the 1970's, with all its windows very darkly tinted. Thor and Barney pressed on but watched in their rearview mirrors that the Cadillac came to a screeching stop, back at the driveway they'd just left. Barney saw four thugs hopping out of the car and putting a bullet into the head of the one-handed guy. Barney stepped on the gas, flooring the truck's accelerator--very reminiscent of the way Thor had done back at the train--and said, "Let's get the Hell out of here!" Thor, taking another look back (but wishing he hadn't) saw the Caucasian girl being choked to death by a guy with a piece of blue fabric, and another one was starting to cut her dress with a knife. Thor wanted to tell Barney, but it came out as "Drive faster!"

CHAPTER 4

It was turning pitch-black outside before they'd reached the Kankakee City Limits, and Thor and Barney needed to observe the Kankakee Nature Center's trail route before doing anything else. Thor feared the thugs might be trying to follow them, which is why he didn't let Barney stop the truck till getting to the Kankakee Nature Center. Barney turned the truck into a restaurant's parking lot, which was next to the Kankakee Trail, and divided it with a chain link fence. Thinking the parking spot was ideal (for where they needed to be anyway) Thor and Barney decided to take a break. Thor decided to run into the restaurant, looking to get something to eat, while Barney thought he'd smoke a joint quickly outside--calm his nerves--before he'd head in the restaurant too. Inside the small diner, Thor saw an open freezer filled with shrimp flavored Ramen noodles. Thor commented out loud "Yuck! No wonder this town's nuts." Then, a cute Oriental lady emerged from the back of the kitchen area and greeted Thor. Her English wasn't perfect, so she asked, "What are you on She Fo?" Thor understood that "She" means market in Chinese, so kept the conversation going by answering "I am in the market for *gulp* shrimp Ramen noodles." The oriental woman bagged it up and pointed to the clock, then said "Hei-ban get to safety!" Thor was lucky the lady had pointed to the clock, because he didn't know "Hei-ban" means blackboard in Chinese, so it would have been impossible to deduce what the HELL she'd meant otherwise; being she'd meant clock but didn't know how to say it herself. Apparently, whatever was coming was coming at a soon time. Barney made his way into the building, saw the Oriental lady with Thor; talking about time being almost midnight, but realized Thor was already ready to leave the restaurant. Barney, not knowing what to do, asked "Should we turn on the Bat-signal?" Barney could sense things seemed like trouble, so just followed Thor and left the restaurant.

Things started making more sense about what was going to happen at midnight, when Thor and Barney got back to their truck. It looked like there was a slight glow coming from inside the Kankakee Trail, but there was also a silver convertible parked by their truck now too, and it was honking its horn at them to come over. There were two guys in the car, one looking like Flavor Flav, and was holding an automatic weapon. Then, the man with the weapon stood up on the cars' seat, as to be sticking out the open convertible roof area, and just stared at Barney and Thor-- most likely trying to figure if they're friend or foe. It wasn't long before the guys in the silver convertible decided Thor and Barney weren't up to no good, so they told Thor and Barney about the same thing the Oriental lady had told them, about getting to safety. Then, the man sitting in the driver's seat of the silver convertible took it a step further, saying "There will be 4 dead suckers coming to the restaurant tonight, and the trail ghosts are starting to get active." The two-guy told Thor and Barney a few details, which helped sum up that there was a vendetta war going on in the small town--stemming from events of the past few years. The guy that looked like Flavor Flav said "Someone was bombing us, we hadn't a gun around to defend ourselves, and my dad was hiding between a rock and a crevice for safety. Nowhere was safe for long, as far as shelter space was concerned, so a few of the townspeople gathered to form a defensive wall; standing up to the opposing menace; but the Hood Thugs had more than deer hunting shotguns, using a Ghetto Blaster to mow down the wall of town people. Hood Thugs came out here and started taking over, place by place, store by store; killing everyone along the way; acting as if killing was a sport. Anyway, my brother snapped (had had enough) and ran out of a safe place, then a boom and a fireball made him no more. This guy (pointing at the driver of the silver convertible) tried putting on a white flag, as if it were a cape, which the thugs took as surrender; therefore, they let him live, but they took his sister hostage anyway. He'd been paying them so they wouldn't hurt her but was unable to pay the last $2,000.00 to get her back. Well, last week her body turned up over there (pointing to the Kankakee Trail), beaten to death and throat slit. We're here for a little retribution . . . just waiting for our targets!"

CHAPTER 5

Thor and Barney realized it was useless in the situation to be hanging around, so both agreed they would head into the Kankakee Nature Center; driving right in, even though it was after hours, and getting the truck out of sight. Being in the parking lot of the restaurant with the truck, they would've been easily recognized by the thugs; especially after what they'd witnessed them do. Besides, after midnight the trail ghosts-- if there were any--would be active and possibly visible, so they'd hoped to catch a glimpse of the paranormal activities. Barney drove and Thor rode shotgun, entering the Kankakee Nature Trail till they were completely out of sight from the road entrance.

The Kankakee Trail ghosts didn't show themselves at first, and Barney kept on driving through the Kankakee Nature Preserve till he was off the far back end of the property, before turning around. Apparently, the far property end was a jurisdiction agreement point (when exactly isn't clear), which expired; a new lot line's draft never being reached or enacted. Just then, the spirits appeared and whizzed past the truck, causing it to stop in its tracks and quit running altogether. A cloud of black smoke was all around once the ghosts went past, which, as it cleared, left cylinders of explosives surrounding the truck on all sides, blocking Thor and Barney from exiting except by foot. Next, the ghosts all appeared and were lying on the ground, seemingly in their normal human form; except that they were translucent. They were the ghosts of all the Kankakee people who'd gone missing the past few years and were crying for justice; even to the level of killing an innocent person (like Barney and/or Thor) to get it.

As it turned out, Barney's friend Cowboy was one of the ghosts. Barney saw Cowboy and a song from a ride at Disney World came to his mind, having a repeating lyric of "It's a small world after all." Barney then remembered when he'd shot a music video with Cowboy, wearing his silly 10-gallon hat, and how everyone got drunk and sang "It's a small world." Now, here was Cowboy, still wearing the hat, and as a ghost! Cowboy made it clear to Barney that all the ghosts wanted was to be destroyed; hoping to end their suffering, which would also cause the daily haunting of the Kankakee Trail to cease. It was a sad day to know that the beautiful trail pathway, amidst the nature park, had become nothing more than a gang's body dumpsite. What the ghosts were requesting, though, was a hard thing to please.

CHAPTER 6

Having now pieced the story together fully, Thor got on his soapbox (he felt a speech coming on), introducing himself to the ghosts as "One who's been known to play Sigmund Freud to family and friends." Thor went for the jugular, starting into a speech that put his years of motivational speaking to the test: "Friends (addressing all the ghosts), utilities advertise along the side of the Interstate with billboards, saying things like 'It's the season again,' but utilities are something everyone uses; so, they have no need to advertise. There are not enough new, daily customers, just now deciding to get electricity, all because they drove past a billboard that said to. If the electric company were to stop advertising so ridiculously, consumer costs could be lowered by the amount of all the wasted advertising costs. We, the consumers, have only one choice for sewer provider, normal mail delivery (USPS), Gas Company, and Water

Company. It is unimaginable that any other company could run a whole separate set of power lines or sewer tunnels to compete with the city, so why waste advertising costs on a war that's already won? Now, I've seen a Jang reptile; it looks a lot like a lizard, but all it did was look for its mother its whole life: Pathetic! The thing never gets its own life together; just one day the Jang reptile takes the place of its deceased relative, and the inhumanity of the cycle continues. The point I'm trying to come to, simply put, is that you're in a town overrun by hoodlums, and running them out of town isn't easy; especially when the town can't even take care of itself. You're expecting justice, but your physical community and the Kankakee land itself is crying for justice too! YOU, the Kankakee Trail Ghosts, have another choice; you're not limited to some kind of life pattern following; you can all pull together to save the land itself from the poison that has moved in. On the way here, I witnessed that very poison (Hood Thugs) murder two more of your friends and neighbors . . . nobody's, just another couple down the road. No! They were a biracial couple and they sold me and my friend some fuel, which without that fuel we would be dead right now too! They, they saved my life (a single tear falls from   Thor's eye in memoriam). Don't you think they're crying for justice too? The way I see it and will proclaim it (being I've driven off the back side of the property), is this trail's jurisdiction line is now completely open to the entire Kankakee Valley--there's no trespass here. GO! Collect up with all the other dearly departed locals, no longer being shackled to this trail, and as a group rid your beautiful land of the beast that's moved upon her. You're GHOSTS for Pete's sake!"

The ghosts realized they'd been acting like Halloween decorations; not like the brave spirits they really were, so decided immediately to do their part; hearing and hearing the call (like they should've). Just as the trail ghosts shook off all the sulking they'd been doing, the Oriental restaurant lady was heard yelling "Help, Hel..." with sounds of shooting piercing the air. The sounds of heavy gunfire came next, ringing from two directions, echoing throughout the darkness in Kankakee Nature Preserve. A clear voice was heard saying "Now for the rest of the money," along with the sounds POP! POP! It was highly evident to Thor, Barney, and the ghosts that the Oriental lady had bitten the dust, and that the guys in the silver convertible had become target practice. The ghosts were beyond pissed at the idea of losing more turf and people to the Hood Thugs, so they stormed off in Army like fashion, going to meet the thugs head on. The ghosts left the Kankakee reservation looking like they'd already won the war, and took all the explosives, along with their new prerogative with them.

CHAPTER 7

Thor and Barney found themselves left alone on the nature trail, in the absolute black of night, and started feeling their way back to the truck. The truck's dome lights came on as soon as they opened the door, indicating that the truck's power was restored too. Thor and Barney heard a whistling sound in the distance, then came a great and ominous HUM*POOM sound. A bright light, looking like a mini version of the August 1945 A-Bomb explosion at Nagasaki, was seen about 40 acres (about twice the area of Chicago's Millennium Park) over from where they were in the truck, so Thor told Barney "That's it, we're getting out of here NOW! Obviously, those ghosts' explosives worked." Then, everything was just absolute stillness. There were the sounds of only the crickets chirping, frogs croaking, and an occasional owl who, playing the song of night-- nothing else or more could be heard. Thor started the truck's motor, which fired right up, and Barney said, "Hit it," wanting to get out of town as quickly as possible himself. As Thor and Barney got to the exit from the trail, heading back out onto the road for home, it became really evident that for the Kankakee Valley "it" was over; peace had been found at last.

The End

JACK GRASP'S DINER STORY

CHAPTER 1

J ack Grasp had a menial job, washing dishes and serving coffee to customers, at a diner called The Steel Palace. He'd worked there for a long time, not worried about his pay so much, as he truly loved everything about the diner, the people, the view, and the uniqueness of the diner's structure. The diner, when it was being built, was made (primarily) from repurposing the galley and stainless-steel kitchen sections of a ship with "questionable" origins, that'd been salvaged at the local marina. After greasing the "right" people's palms (it's not known what was all used, but people swear it wasn't just money), the diner's owner obtained the ship's sections, hoping to create an establishment with a nostalgic feel, yet original character charm: It Worked! Jack Grasp was a bit of a maverick, envisioning his own creative ideas enhancing the diner's looks too; noting while visiting the Northeastern Coast a restaurant, made from what looked like a 1950's

Airstream trailer, having neon lights on its front-side that read DINER. Jack suggested The Steel Palace should also be aglow in neon lights, protruding from the roof like billboards, spread out along the diner's port and starboard sides. The diner's owner didn't agree, answering why not by flat-out aiming to put Jack's thoughts into the ash heap; telling him to "Get a grip Grasp," along with a derogatory comment about Jack probably seeing a "Trailer Park in Harlem" and quoted something they'd heard on TV about "Blame who's to blame, for what's to blame for!"

Be all that as it may, Jack held to his "Beautiful as an Autumn Day" viewpoint about the Steel Palace Diner, though local citizens referred to it as "The Hull" and crafted some wild conspiracy theories (more or less) about the place's legal origins. If legend's correct, some old government ships' parts were used in building The Steel Palace, however, they weren't cleared for unauthorized use; still containing serial numbers and things, and as such were still "active" parts, within zones and limits. Somehow or another, the diner was able to maintain a civilian boating license, having made a counter seating area from seam-welding a ships' lower-deck workbenches together; thus, creating a structural "beam." The typical restaurant stools, usually set with dining counters, weren't happening at The Steel Palace; instead, the counter area had swivel seats that were harvested from ships' pilot houses. If The Steel Palace happened to be floating away--like from a dam breaking and a flood washing the diner away--anyone sitting in a chair at the counter would, technically, be its Captain (or Captain's) and in command of trying to either "right or abandon ship." As for locals who called the diner "The Hull," it was really a sign of respect; most folks believed that if a boat motor were attached to The Steel Palace, and the whole place had been launched in the water, it could sail a short distance! If the diner did ever sail, it would be in Pirate, because in the kitchen there's an old 1939 Hobart dishwasher that never got "cleared" yet had been pulled from an old Warship. Looking at the thing, it's evident the dishwasher was on the opposite side of a bulkhead from a munition's locker room; external burn marks indicated a direct hit must've been taken.

CHAPTER 2

Jack's no slouch with his own theories (conspiracy or otherwise) either, finding something questionable in most, if not all, subject matters. Heck, if there's one reason the local Old Guys Group even came to the Steel Palace Diner, it's to hear Jack's latest theory. The Old Guys enjoyed sitting at the diner's counter and sharing their thoughts on his thoughts; sometimes the topics even held merit--though, it's possible, going to the diner just got them out of their houses and away from their old ladies for a little while. Armond, who's known by Arm for short, lived in an apartment across the road from The Steel Palace and would go there often for coffee, as well as to converse with everybody; he knew all the locals: Old Guys, Jack, the diner's owner, Jack's girlfriend, etc.; priding himself with the ability to know when an "out of towner" was present. Arm had been flabbergasted the first time he'd walked into the diner and heard Jack telling a woman his theory on how the "pink tax" was a government ploy to keep the population controlled, if only by keeping women poorer than men; forcing them to spend more for the same goods, therefore stopping them from having currency enough to comfortably enjoy spreading their legs, else having fears of living poorer by baby making a costly female child. Armond thought, then interjected himself in the discussion, which is when/how he first met Jack--unbeknownst that he was interrupting Jack teasingly talking to his long-term girlfriend. Arm stated "JFK didn't pull out! Nobody would! Marilyn Monroe was too sexy for him to have. The government rubbed her out because if she talked to the press (regarding the affair) the American people would believe her, no matter what, over anything JFK ever said. Marilyn Monroe, smash or pass--that's the story TIME Magazine should've went with. By silencing Marilyn, the government attempted to deny it happened."

Arm was the kind of guy who still flew a 48-star USA flag out his window, which worked, but looked a little weird. Arm had watched every episode of DR. WHO since '63 and was always telling people how just 20 years before the show started, back in '43, after he got through the US Army's training camp, he was stationed with the British (allied forces) when FDR declared war on the European Powers (Germany and Italy), and that that show had the exact same sci-fi mentality "those BBC guys" had, even back then. Jack became friends with Arm within seconds of meeting each other, and Arm realized how to "pull Jack's strings" just as quickly; especially if he was needing a refill, as he was a coffee hound; blurting out some random government involved babble "Government censorship! That's why I isn't getting as many letters as I used to. I tell you, I found out what's wrong!" That was like a whistle to a dog in Jack's ears; causing him to come in a hurry.

CHAPTER 3

J ack Grasp and Armond got on the topic of discussing a noticeable imbalance in one's own personal defenses, completely unlike any expected surprise events (tornados, train derailments, fires, etc.), where a person that's planning to do someone or something harm has the natural upper hand; using the art of surprise attack to achieve a "win," if only on the small scale, 90% of the time, vs. a large attack which (usually) fails 70+% of the time; the more people involved, the more chance of someone talking, as well as the more chance for foul-up's. Arm was saying "Realistically, in today's society, a large-scale surprise attack is 99.999% impossible. Though I like nothing more than repeating one's own words back to them when they're incorrect, even if it's years later, and having them claim 'I don't think I ever said that' though knowing they damn well did. It makes me laugh! Oh, to think Jack, one day repeating your words back to you...

you couldn't possibly be correct." Jack knew Arm was just scared and chattering off the topic, as it could be true of any war, any time, so he laid it out easy for Arm, saying "You still feel the USA is fixed from being vulnerable! If I were just 1 person--not someone on the watch list, mind you-- in each of the 50 states, having sick mind and a vendetta, couldn't I easily 'do in' at least 1 random, unsuspecting at lunch break, American; that's easy math, equaling at least 50 casualties."

The discussion went deep, Jack and Arm each going back 'n forth about the "art" of surprise attack, when Arm stated that in the latest episode of Doctor Who, the TARDIS (Time And Relative Dimension(s) in Space) was mistaken in its coordinates and the Police Phone Box landed upside down on top of The Doctor., which then reminded him of a scene in The Wizard of OZ, somehow with the Wicked Witch getting flattened by a house. Jack was completely confused and thought Arm really needs to get out more. As it was his turn to reply, Jack continued towards making his point "The person in the back of a room gets less noticed. It's my 'Distance Back Theory.' At a concert everyone watches the entertainer, so whoever's standing behind everyone (back row, in the cheap seats) could be watching the back of everyone's head, as well as the show. If the guy/gal in the back of a room ducks out, it usually goes unnoticed; whereas if a member of the main act runs off stage, everybody will notice, because everyone was facing the performer in the first place. Worse yet, if the person in back is a Foreign Country, trying on purposely to be of little notice in overtaking change; any 'progress' they make may be undetectable, especially if done slowly (over time) enough." Arm started talking about how the female 13th Doctor's shows, in the Doctor Who series, had done poorly in the ratings (vs. the previous 12 male doctors' ratings), having the BBC declare them '...worst in the last 36 years.' Arm was describing some ideas for an Under doggy style to come up from behind, when Jack cut him off, reminding Arm he shouldn't say "Doggy style come from behind," in any capacity, stating "The Hell's wrong with you!?" when talking about a proper British lady. Then, Jack continued with his 'Behind Theory' logic, saying "China's printing out play money, which denotes different American currency values; to be used by kids in learning to count change, and for playing with in their games. You can buy a 'play money' kit (containing paper dollars and plastic coins) from any Dollar Store, though big chain stores sell them too. Now, sticking with the Dollar Store, where everything (for the most part) should cost a dollar + the State sales tax, though Counties and cities can charge an additional local sales tax of up to 0.6%, for a maximum possible combined sales tax of 5.6%. I want to again note: There is no way that this fake cash should be assumed to be real currency; it should be viewed as 100% non-valuable to everyone! Now, here's the stinger--if I've done my math correctly. During the actual point of sale (adding in the sale price, plus taxes) the fake, plastic, made in China penny in a 'play money' kit becomes worth more than an actual minted in the USA penny! To say China is making 2 cents of real money on every fake 1 cent coin sold is an understatement!" Arm made a mental note to "borrow" his nephew's play money that he'd bought him one Christmas.

CHAPTER 4

Tracy Bedart was Jack's girlfriend and worked at The Tavern, next-door to The Steel Palace diner. She could hear Jack's voice reverberating through the wall-way, betwixt the two establishments, sounding a lot like the Charlie Brown teachers' "Wah" voice and was trying to decipher what he was complaining about now. Though both establishments established their own policies on what activities customers must follow, an ovular shaped hatchway door a decommissioned Navy ship's bulkhead separated both businesses (The Tavern from the diner); originally, it's purpose was training Semen in quickly making K-type shoring (out of wood, tied together with rope) if a bulkhead (wall) got damaged at Sea; allowing water to fill up along the wall in a simulated flood environment. Because the storage room was a total afterthought to the building's design plan, and because The Diner's owner knew a guy that knew a guy, the wall was somehow harvested from an official Navy training site that was remodeling. Using the bulkhead wall as a go-between to the two room sections when the building was initially being built really sealed The Steel Palace Diner's ship appearance, though doing nothing for the storage area next door, which later became The Tavern. The hatchway door opened out toward what was the storage room; keeping it from getting in the pathway of diner customers and/or employees, but, when it didn't get used because the diner didn't have anything to store, the owner decided to sell the room. With the storage room's sale to a man named Rolland, The Tavern was born. Oddly, because the wall was never really decommissioned, any time commissioned officers where in the bulkhead's presence (if they were aware) they'd be able to take official actions to caliber levels of happening on live Government quarters; kind of a "Fines Double in Work Zones!" treatment--the way police may fine civilian speeders in construction areas. Anyway, Tracy, hearing Jack talking, decided to make a trip over to the diner, so, taking a $20 bill she yelled to her boss "We're low on singles! I'm going to see if the diner can make change for a twenty-dollar bill." With that, Tracy giggled and took a Smirnoff Vodka's advertising balloon off the wall-way, then made her way into the diner via the little used hatchway; trying to get the jump on Jack.

Sneaking up on Jack would be about impossible for anyone except Tracy, as Jack really watched his surroundings and others watched his surroundings too for whatever he might be watching for. Tracy was Jack's heart and everybody knew it, so as the powers be, she had the ability of roaming Mother Nature level natural around Jack; free of anything that might be questioned by anyone in the slightest; just as 2 magnets facing each other correctly will automatically pull themselves together, normally with great force, slamming and holding each other tightly together; Jack never allowed anything, or anybody, to reverse turn one of them--at least no one that still enjoys oxygen. Just as Jack said "Satellite Shoot" to Armond, Tracy snuck up behind Jack and popped her balloon, creating a hollow popping echo to ring throughout The Steel Palace diner. Arm and Jack were both startled and Arm even turned ghost white for a moment; the echo still ringing reminding Arm of the TARDIS landing in the Doctor Who show. With big eyes, Tracy giggled and watched Jack catch his breath, but then he cast her back a smile that made her feelings go beyond the joy levels; like they'd been apart so long and finally had time to make life, though they were only apart a few hours. Tracy asked Jack if he could make change for the $20 bill and Jack just kissed her cheek while nodding, then took the $20 and headed for the register. Arm, meanwhile, heard someone slurring the words "Little Debbie," which's what the drunks at The Tavern had nicknamed Tracy. All the sudden, there was a man (though not much of a man) slumping halfway in the diner and halfway in The Tavern with his Svedka Vodka drink in his left hand. Arm approached the individual and made him hold his drink in his right hand; the diner has rules about no alcohol on its premises, so the man could either oblige and keep the drink in his other hand, or else 1/2 of him would get banned from ever entering the diner again. The slumping guy got really confused when Tracy and Arm tried explaining how if he "Needed to be thrown out of The Steel Palace diner, he'd have to be thrown into The Tavern first as he was legally only half thrown out of the diner." The man started thinking he was cut in half about the time Jack came back, giving Tracy her change. Tracy kissed Jack on the cheek and said "Thanks!!!" Jack then approached the man, who now was leaning upright, kind of, propped against the doorway's bulkhead. Jack asked the man why he thought it was a good idea to call Tracy "Little Debbie," to which the guy said "Burp, Great Gatsby, burp. Ha, Steel Palace Diner! The Hull. Ah, Little Debbie has nice cookies, ha-ha. She's a nice cookie." Jack immediately helped the intoxicated guy move his drink back over to his left hand, being that arm was on the diner's side; then Jack proceeded to throw the man into The Tavern, yelling out to The Tavern's Owner "Rolland, come get your drunken client, or I'm putting him in your car!" Meanwhile, Arm asked Tracy "How often do they call you that?" to which Tracy simply answered, "When they get drunk, customers hound me for everything; reasons unimaginable."

CHAPTER 5

J ack came back to Arm and Tracy after tending to the drunk guy fiasco, and he could tell Tracy was interested in knowing what "Satellite Shoot" meant, just by the look on her face; Tracy was very inquisitive when it came to all things Jack, also her eyebrows stayed raised when she held back a question, making it pretty obvious: she wondered. To help explain how the subject got to where it was, Arm mentioned to Tracy what Jack had told him about the "Distance Back Theory," to which Tracy replied "Oh, like how staying in the back of crowds is easier for passing through; there's much less interaction with people containing you! The front and middle rows are a real pain in the neck, and security is always tightest up front by the main act. If that's it, what you're saying must be true, I guess." Arm started to feel dumb because he hadn't even understood it that well hearing it from Jack, though little did he know Tracy had heard bits & pieces of Jack's theory earlier while she was quietly sneaking into the diner from The Tavern.

Jack realized Tracy needed to get back over to The Tavern, so he tried to sum it all up: "Satellite Shoot is based off of the Distance Back Theory; without knowing the Distance Back Theory it would be almost impossible to explain the other. Taking your people at a concert example, which I'd also used earlier--Great mind's think alike--while 99% of the audience is watching the main act, including some of the security detail; let's get real, like they wouldn't get distracted and take a good look if Stevie Ray Vaughn was making Blues Music History (playing faster than anyone ever or something) live and in concert?! Of course, security would be watching in awe, and it's in that moment of not watching that the unnoticed individual with ill intent makes his move, creeping to his perfect location." At that moment Tracy realized she needed to run the singles she'd gotten in change from the $20, back over to The Tavern, and while there tell her boss that she'd like to take her lunch break; the topic was getting interesting, and Tracy wanted to make sure she got to hear and understand it all.

As soon as Tracy walked back into The Tavern, she realized her boss hadn't even noticed she wasn't back yet; after getting too tangled up with trying to throw the 1/2 way in 1/2 way out guy 1/2 way out in the street, leaving him out in front of The Tavern and The Steel Palace diner. Tracy's boss shouted for her to "Shut the hatchway," so she yelled to Jack "Order me a burger and fries. You and Arm have a coffee on me, I'll be right back." With that, The Tavern owner helped her push the hatchway closed. By the time Tracy had left The Tavern, walked the short distance of outside sidewalk over to the diner and come through the front door, she saw Jack and Arm relaxing in the Captain's Chairs at the counter, enjoying their coffees, and her food order was already ready and waiting, though somehow a couple of her fries had made their way onto Jack's placemat.

Tracy sat down by her plate and said to Jack "Ok, let me get this straight. You're implying that the guy with the cheapest seat is somehow Lording over everyone, including the main act mind you; acting as if he/she's some sort of religious zealot!?" Before Jack got into the deepest extremities of an answer, he first suggested to Tracy, he'd show her why being behind is better, in a private experiment between them at his apartment later. Tracy understood the message and giggled. Now, Tracy was listening, and Arm was listening mighty intently too, so Jack went for the real answer saying "You're only right till you're wrong. Dead Wrong! In this case let's recall all the holes in racetrack and ballpark fences throughout history. Young boys sneaking a peek at their heroes of NASCAR or Baseball; no one, police or otherwise, patrol the farthest off peek-hole with the same tenacity as the inner track or field. Now, let's chance the course of history; it's 1928 and someone takes a rifle to the unpatrolled hole on game day, but instead of watching the ball game he/she shoots Babe Ruth in the heart while he's at the pitcher's mound; using a rifle scope at 500+

yards . . . so it goes. No, if someone did that in Babe's prime, there would damn well be police patrolling the outermost fencing probably better than the front row. It's absurd! Why must the worst always occur before people see the problem? And to think, security is paid highly just to line the way down a tunnel to the ball player's locker room. That same guy who'd shoot through a fence hole could pay $3,000 dollars for a front row seat and never be able to cock the gun's hammer, while for no money he/she can waste a team through a hole in a fence. At a concert it's the same thing, everyone's trying to rush to the stage, attempting to get as close as they can, meanwhile security is tied up keeping people back in their place. Now comes the guy with ill intent, cheap back row creeping, choosing anyone in the audience that he/she may want to destroy with a back of the head shot. Of course, they will only get 1 or 2 shots and be noticed, but by the time the jig's up they've achieved their goal already." Arm and Tracy got chills just thinking about it, and then jinxed each other saying "The Hell, Jack! What does that have to do with Satellites?" Jack took a sip of his coffee, savoring it as he looked seriously at Arm, then at Tracy, not saying anything; just letting the thought of what he'd said sink in and their brains before speaking again. Suddenly, Arm and Tracy gasped in unison as an answer crept into their minds. Jack said "Good, now you're getting it. While the satellites are in some sort of alignment in orbit, doing their regular broadcasting or charting from what's been deemed an 'ideal placement zone' in space, someone like Russia would have placed one out farther away; thus, behind and away from everything of any normal use. Sure, it's Lording over the other satellites of every other country that's in orbit; doing nothing other than just mapping where every other satellite is moving in space and what country the units are from. It doesn't need to function well like the other satellites, which are up there doing a service for mankind, as it just is there to 'watch' everyone else's; much like they're all just the back of heads of an audience." Tracy and Arm both double jinxed each other, exclaiming "Holy Shit!" Jack just toyed with them after that, saying "That's just the basics of Satellite Shoot with Distance Back Theory. Rocking in the USSR, in the USA...Crosshairs over the United States-- Comrades, Informants--Red Airwaves--Boom. Tracy and Arm left the diner having suspicions about everyone they saw, for the rest of the evening.

CHAPTER 6

The Tavern was owned by a man named Rolland. He had boughten the old storage room from the diner's owner, making it into The Tavern by adding: a front door, some windows, heat and water, but when he started poking around during remodeling, it became apparent how cheaply the diner's owner had constructed the room (being an afterthought in the first place), being it wasn't built with salvaged ship's materials; in fact it was built with highly questionable resources, as to even being structural goods. The Tavern's owner realized too late that he'd have been better off just tearing down and rebuilding, disconnecting from The Steel Palace in the process. It would cost him more money in the long run, modifying fixes and re-adapting things; trying to turn the room into something that could be open safely to the public, rather than just starting over from scratch. Now, because the diner was such a special insurance circumstance, possibly being a fire hazard to itself; having been running 115v power through some (if not most) of the old ship's wiring, although it was really unlabeled military coaxial cable which, surprisingly, kept on working fine, and with Rolland's establishment structurally butted against it, insurance costs for The Tavern were 3 times what every other bar in the area was paying. After a short time, Rolland started to despise The Diner's owner for even building something so shoddy--learning the hard way why people (usually) have an inspection done before purchasing real estate.

Rolland had been part of a demolition squad in WW2, equipped with flame throwers, bazookas, machine guns, heavier mortars, blocks of TNT (weighing 1 pound each) used as a satchel charge 25-30 blocks at a time, 105 Long Toms, and was involved in most (if not all) of the toughest fighting with the Japanese. He claims "All I did was mix up flamethrower fuel and repair bazookas . . . send the guy's explosives. I got combat credit for Noemfoor Island because I joined the outfit just a day before the operation. I didn't see any action on The Stars and Stripes." Rolland was standing on the sidewalk, unlocking The Tavern's front door, when Arm came strolling by--in his head saying "damn it" when he noticed Rolland--making his way over to the diner. Rolland gestured for a handshake to the passing Arm; therefore, roping Armond into listening to him for a minute. Arm shook Rolland's hand, saying "Good morning' Roll! Keeping it all in line!?" making Rolland wonder if Arm noticed The Tavern had shifted away from the sidewalk a little; a noticeable gap of 1/2" is now where the sidewalk had been tight against the building before winter. Roland made a *humph* like sound, then advised Arm "You got to be more like those ack-ack boys," mimicking the sounds the supporting aircraft guns made when he'd heard them in WW2 "and stop them from censoring your personal mail!" after hearing about Arm's little blurting rant, over at the diner. Arm replied "The damn rumors are going around here like hotcakes! I didn't . . . so long." Rolland laughed and watched Arm scurrying away toward the diner, repeating "I didn't . . . hotcakes."

Tracy arrived at The Tavern for work after a lousy night's sleep, recalling Jack's story from the previous day. Rolland, sweeping cigarette butts off the sidewalk out front the Tavern, saw Tracy arrive for work and asked, "How's that bastard down the road?" He was referring to the owner of The Steel Palace Diner, but Tracy thought he was referring to Jack Grasp and replied "He's a chicken stuck in a wall kind of guy;" she'd been waiting all week for Jack to ask her out to a movie on the weekend and was frustrated that he hadn't yet. Rolland, assuming Tracy was referring to the diner's owner, was more than happy to agree with her analogy and offered her a .50 cent raise.

CHAPTER 7

Jack had propped the front door of The Steel Palace open, letting some fresh morning air in, and had heard Rolland laughing and Arm saying something, so he decided to step outside and see what the word was. Jack saw Arm just standing there, looking dejected at the ground, and realized Rolland must've really gotten to him. Jack had nothing going on and decided it was time for Rolland to go inside The Tavern, if all he was going to do was bully customers heading to The Diner. Before he said anything to Arm, Jack looked up momentarily at the Sun, causing himself to force a sneeze--by some fluke of nature; he'd naturally reacted that way to looking quickly at the sun his whole life. Because Jack was outside, he didn't cover his mouth, letting the open sneeze fly; though, being courteous enough to turn his head, so as not to sneeze on Arm, but wound up sending the sneeze in the general direction of The Tavern and Rolland, who was still standing outside putzing around.

Rolland claimed he felt Jack's sneeze spray him and shouted "God Damn it, Jack! Jackass! Cover your lousy mouth!" Jack took the liberty of walking over to Rolland at that point, confronting him and planning to "correct" the sneeze as being a dirty misconception--it may have lengthened Rolland's life instead, and so the sneeze shouldn't be cursed at. Arm, meanwhile, ducked out into the diner. Jack asked Rolland "Haven't you ever heard of the Driver-Passenger Relationship Theory?" Rolland, being upset, growled "No, I haven't." Jack wasn't about to excuse his own sneeze; in fact, he felt it quite rude that Rolland didn't give him a gesundheit. Jack said "Rolland, you'd agree that men usually drive when a man and woman are in a vehicle together, right? And isn't it a fact, when a person's driving a vehicle alone and has a sneeze coming faster than they could grab a napkin (or something), they typically turn their head (especially in Winter and Summer; car's windows frozen shut, or Air Conditioning is running) toward the empty passenger side of the vehicle; avoiding spraying the windshield in front of them, instead sending the offending sneezing all over the empty passenger area. Now, I don't know about you, but I don't want to sit in the passenger seat unless I know the person cleans their car daily; norovirus can live on hard or soft surfaces for about two weeks, as if that isn't scary enough." Rolland was trying to figure out where Jack was going with this and started to listen with interest. Jack continued, knowing he need to drill the point soon "The driver, who's most likely the owner of the vehicle, has--more likely than not--been loosely sneezing all over the car interior while driving for so long that the passenger's side is disgusting; grab a microscope for more proof. By the next time they have a passenger sitting in their car, they've forgotten about cleaning (unless they're a UBER driver, who's learned all about cleaning between passengers) the passenger side; instead choosing to converse with the person, maybe even swinging through a Mc Donald's drive-thru; getting some to-go food and eating it in the car. Meanwhile, not knowing that everything in the automobile's been sneeze sprayed by a pig of an owner, the unsuspecting passenger winds up touching things in the vehicle: door handle, ash tray, seat belt, seat levers, maybe the radio console to change out Cd's; then handles the fast food they've just bought and eats. Yummy, germs!" At this point Rolland was grossed out; being he'd never done anything but vacuum his car and his wife and kid were always in it. Rolland hesitated as to what Jack's point was when Jack said "Passengers outlive drivers, crashes and such excluded from this statement; a.k.a. women outlive men. The germy sneeze is the only thing in the passenger seat till an actual passenger comes along, who 80% of the time winds up out living the driver, a.k.a. man." Rolland felt queasy for even listening to Jack's theory and went inside The Tavern. Jack, having succeeded in getting Rolland off the sidewalk, headed back to The Diner, finding Arm waiting like a dog for its owner, hounding by the entrance door. Jack just said, "You're welcome."

CHAPTER 8

The owner of The Steel Palace Diner had a habit of wearing a new dress and coming to work early on payday Fridays, supposedly to hand out the employee's checks ASAP, but some people knew there was a little more make-up to it; this was one of those days. The diner received its weekly groceries delivery on Mondays, and the lunch crowd was busiest on Friday's, though the menu had had the same choices all week. Tracy walked the sidewalk over to the diner while taking a break from The Tavern, thinking about what foods they'd have that she might want to eat for lunch, when the owner of the diner saw her and asked "Can I leave Jack's paycheck with you? You can give it to him if and when you see him." Leaving Jack's paycheck with Tracy was just like asking her to open it and see what Jack earned that week; she couldn't resist peeking at it. The diner's owner said "He (Jack) spends 8 hours a day here, but I'm lucky to make any money on the coffee he sells to the group of guys that usually come here; they buy their cup-o-Joe, which comes with free refills, and they just sit there--sometimes for hours on end--drinking refills till the coffee pot becomes empty. You do the math! I tell you, when Jack's having a coffee with the customers himself and being social, he never pushes them to buy any food!" Tracy reminded the owner "Jack's really a dishwasher. What have you been expecting? He doesn't even remember to ask me out, though we're dating; acting all like he's got options." At that, the diner's owner and Tracy started laughing together hysterically.

Jack made his way over to the diner owner's office space, barely sectioned away from the cash register area, where he wasn't too surprised when seeing Tracy and the owner chuckling away at his expense. Jack at least understood how his pay might be a source of amusement to his girlfriend, but when it came to the owner of The Steel

Palace, who it was pretty obvious was having one of their "Pink Days"--not that that changed the fact "clocking" the diner's owner wasn't difficult--, had no reason to laugh about paying an employee twice the going wage rate for the job; leaving Jack feeling like an amusement object being watched. Jack assumed Tracy had probably seen his paycheck and in his best British accent, while trying to be swanky, said "Well, Ms. Bedart, when you're Mrs. Grasp and looking at those figures it may not be so funny." Tracy's laughing turned into her giggling again. Tracy handed Jack his paycheck and Jack stopped the accent. Then, Jack whispered to her "By the way, we're going to The Olive Garden for dinner before hitting up a movie at the Marcus Theater tonight. It might rain, so you'd better run home after work and pack a weekend bag, make sure to add a bathing suit too; we're to get picked up later. I've gotten us a limo rental and hotel reservations out of town this weekend; our sweet has its own pool on the roof." Tracy exclaimed "Oh, Jack, don't tease," to which Jack started to produce tickets from his apron pocket, saying "Surprised? That's not all, I Know you like Cirque du Soleil, so I snagged us a couple tickets; they threw in a few extra freebies for booking out a month in advance." Both Tracy and the diner owner's mouths dropped open, Tracy's heart melted another degree, and Jack kissed her on the forehead before turning around and headed back to do his kitchen duties. As Jack used his setting walking away, he insinuated something about the limo, possibly just picking them up after work, with a clearly shouted "I Love You, Hun!" reply, coming both from the diner Owner and Tracy!

CHAPTER 9

J ack made it a point to wash his hands in the washroom before going back to the kitchen. He'd seen first-hand, growing up, the lack of hand washing education society applies in a normal day; noticing that his own father would go to use the bathroom, then when he was done he'd open the bathroom door with his dirtied potty hands, dragging germs and bacteria across the house out to the kitchen where he'd wash his hands; though sometimes he skipped it and would just go sit in his recliner picking his nose and handling the TV remote. Jack realized the dirt was accumulating under his dad's fingernails and wound up reporting his father to people that could take care of him, as he wasn't taking care of himself properly anymore. Being disgusted with his father, Jack was easily set on the path of being a hand-washing example for people. While standing in the bathroom and looking in the mirror above the sink, Jack saw: his nametag pinned straightly to his apron, his shirt and pants ironed neatly, his shoes clean and new looking, hair combed like Nikola Tesla's and his eyes were well rested. Jack took a moment to reflect on things he'd done in his 42 years of life; priding himself, right or wrong, usually differing when others were relating to social topics; coining it the "Relate, Differ, Relate Method." Jack made it his duty in life to keep "Contrary to popular belief" social upheaval alive.

When it came to the restaurant, Jack was proud to have helped build up the customer base through the years, thinking a sale's a sale and that's money in the bank. Usually, if the coffee didn't sell within an hour's time of being brewed it had to be dumped, and Jack wound up tossing more unused hours' worth of junk coffee away than The Steel Palace Diner actually sold; serving old burnt coffee wouldn't make customers to want to return; which's why people avoided buying the way cooked, 6-hour old, tar-like coffee substance in the pot at the local gas station. The Owner never realized that the daily repeat customers, who came for coffee, weren't there because of the diner's nice appearance--they could've just as easily gone to George Webb's, sat for long stretches of time, just as status seekers and became known as "Webb Rats." No, they came because they truly enjoyed the camaraderie of people from the area (Jack, Tracy, Arm, Rolland, etc.). The Old Guys made up 90% of the diner's coffee clientele, coming by almost daily because they liked Jack and hearing what the "Theory of the Day" was, while sitting with their coffees and sharing their thoughts on his thoughts. Jack looked forward to his next cup of coffee with them. Jack emerged from the washroom, still drying his hands with paper-toweling from the washroom; for show, making it known to anyone looking that he'd most certainly washed them (lest anyone wonder).

CHAPTER 10

The Old Guys were in the diner, sitting comfortably in the Captains' and First Mates' chairs all along the stainless-steel counter, waiting patiently to be served and discussing if any of them heard their favorite AM radio station mention rain coming. One of the Old Guy's Group had fallen asleep, but it didn't change the initial conversation's dynamic enough to notice. The old guy sitting midway down the counter had once been a wrestler, going by the name Moonshine, and had created several different punishing moves, though one was deemed unallowable for use in the sport, which he called "The Hillbilly Hay bailer;" it was this move that got him banned for life from wrestling. Whenever he talked the other old guys usually just stopped whatever they were saying and listened to him, remembering seeing Moonshine's insidious "Hillbilly Hay bailer" move applied once to an opponent. Viewing the move on an old 16mm (about 0.63 in) film, it seemed like Moonshine had turned his body into a John Deere Tractor; turning his arms like implement forks, literally spinning and rolling the opponent up like a bale of hay, then tying a band around him to hold him rolled. Once he was done tilling the poor guy like a field, he'd sit atop the "bail" and drink a glass of moonshine (he used beer). Anyway, Moonshine asked the other old guys "Has anyone seen that crazy self-driving car they've been showing on the news?" The question caused a younger couple sitting at a nearby booth to *Sigh* loudly, while asking to be moved to another table. The old guy sitting at the end of the counter went into a coughing spell and the other old guys answered Moonshine with typical I's and Nay's responses as if the question was being put to a meeting vote. Everyone in the diner clearly heard that the I's had more votes.

Jack, seeing he had The Old Guy's Group waiting at the counter, grabbed two pots of freshly brewed regular coffee: carrying one in each hand, applying the rule of working smarter, not harder. He knew none of the guys would be drinking decaf, so he didn't bother taking it too--seriously, these guys didn't even smoke filtered cigarettes, they sure as Hell weren't worrying about their caffeine intake. All the old guys were waiting patiently with their place settings' coffee mugs turned upwards (vs. upside down, meaning no coffee), creamers all opened and poured into their empty mugs, to "make" the coffee mix with it when poured. These guys were real time savers alright, dirtying a spoon anyway while stirring their coffees before taking a sip--old force of habit and needing to hear a spoon clunk when stirring a coffee mug made them do it. While Jack hit every upturned mug with regular coffee, he asked if anyone wanted decaf, resulting in an unsurprising in unison reply of "Nay!" from not only the Old Guy's Group, but everyone else in The Steel Palace Diner too.

CHAPTER 11

J ack Poured himself a cup o' Joe, deciding to relax with the old guys and talk about the self-driving car issue, and like a dog following its master, Arm moved over to a closer seat too. Jack started off the discussion with "The self-driving car will sell better than expected, and not just in America, for reasons other than merely private citizen transportation, commercial, civil defense, industrial and the like. Not that I've looked at the statistics lately, but there is an untapped percentile of the World's Population that hasn't been able to operate/own a motor vehicle, legally that is, due to some silly reasons. In the USA, a perfectly healthy 20-year-old who's deaf can't get a driver's license, yet an 80-year-old with questionable vision can! There are people with limited mobility issues that a self-driving vehicle would be a cheaper alternative to whatever they're doing currently. Heck, if a 14-year-old kid can fly a remote-control plane or operates a big enough to ride in RC car, some of which are large as real automobiles; certainly, being just as deadly if crashed through a motorist's windshield, maybe we need to look at lowering the driving age, regarding using a self-driving car?! Too, there's some people who are limited special needs adults, meaning they are very capable individuals with an adult level of 5th grade intelligence, whose elderly parents wind up having to drive them everywhere, for life! Depending on what the field is, these same limited special needs people at their job's may work harder than people who aren't special needs at all, and the government makes them pay taxes just like everybody else, so why not let them have a vehicle that could 'help' them to be just like everybody else?! What about the guy with a DUI who's willing to 'pay anything' for another chance at being a motorist...or the veteran who lost everything for the American people, who might be able to make his trip using a self-driving car, otherwise he couldn't."

Arm and The Old Guy's Group chewed on what Jack had said, reflecting on some of the stunts the "Big Three" (Chevy, Ford and Chrysler) had deceived the public within years past. One old guy reminded everybody "Logical people can still be gullible, if and when a corporation is good at chicanery (being deceitful). Moonshine said, "I've heard they're already running them to make pizza deliveries." The comments kept flowing as the sleeping old guy chimed in with "I've had plenty of battery powered electronics that've been squirrelly when their power's getting low; therefore, I'm sure leery of being behind that thing at 60mph if/when its' battery gets low or dies, especially if it just dead-stops." Moonshine came again with "There is no panacea (cure all) vehicle, and every corporation shapes some competitive model of theirs after the latest, greatest, body design some other automotive manufacturer has." The coughing man started working toward saying something, but his coughing spell won, so Jack interjected with the fact that "The prescience (foreknowledge) of automotive styles and features doesn't mean the buying public will be happy with the creature outcome; mixing and blending all those different systems together." Arm couldn't help but say "The first Doctor Who episode in the 2020 season showed a self-driving car that was hacked and hijacked, taking the Doctor and her mates on a wild ride. And like Jack said, there's the liquor factor; inebriated people having slower response, so if you add that to a bad low charged battery, it may well be like deploying a full-blown drunk onto the roadway! Most people don't look at their car's battery every day, or check their oil often enough, that's why we have jumper cables and tow trucks. Don't forget about the asshat who just doesn't care and will transcend the law (go beyond it), somehow conning a jump from anyone they can, just to drive around on a dead battery anyway." Everyone sat silent, sipping their coffees while digesting the slew of comments, but it was the thought of a pizza that really crossed everyone's mind. Jack made a mental note to tell the owner that that's $85 dollars' worth of pizza sales missed out on, not having the type of food the people wanted on the diner's menu.

Jack needed to refill everyone's coffee, including his own, as he was still on the clock and working, working hard or hardly working! If Jack was social with the customers, no one would accuse him of slacking off (not out loud anyway). The Old Guy's Group felt like they were solving the World's upcoming problems, really getting jazzed up to continue the topic when Jack got back. It had started raining outside again, and the couple that had switched tables earlier was done with lunch, making their way out from the diner to an Uber van pulling up out front to pick them up, causing everyone in the diner to watch through the front window when, just as fast as the couple climbed into the Uber van, the Uber's driver threw them back out. Apparently, the woman was ranting about Jack and The Old Guy's Group as "The representation of everything bad," continuing to yell pointlessly at Uber driver, shouting "Honest to God, how do they get away with doing a thing like that?!" The Uber driver was the son of Moonshine and didn't like what the woman was saying about his dad's friends, so as the woman ranted, he just closed and locked the van's doors, shooing away the woman and her useless boyfriend back out into the rain, saying only "Growth and Expansion Reformation" to them before pulling away. The Steel Palace's Owner saw it all go down and decided that if Uber didn't want them, the couple flat-out wouldn't be allowed back in the diner-- not that anyone witnessing the event would've let them back in anyway--so when they tried to come back in, the Diner's Owner swatted them back into the rainy street, saying "Go on, Get!" chasing and swinging at them with one of his high heel shoes. People over at The Tavern, not knowing the story, assumed they were seeing a lover's triangle gone badly.

CHAPTER 12

The man sitting at the end of the counter started having another coughing spell, but this time he pointed a finger to Jack and the Old Guy's, as if to say, "Hold me a place here, bear with me just a moment." Everyone waited, wondering what the man's voice sounded like if he was to speak; the guys had a side bet going that the coughing guy was Irish, and some thought German. When the man finally spoke, he was clearly spoken and addressed everyone with "Gentlemen, I am sure you all know Tracy; the lovely lady who's dating Mr. Grasp here. Well, I'm her father. Our family, in the old country, was once a victim of entailment; meaning the property had to go to a male heir, but Great-Great-Grandpa had only had 5 daughters. Talk about Government interjection between role and function! Let me try to un-blur the line as to this self-driving car bit. The automated vehicle idea has been in man's dreams for longer than the car was even around;

think ability to fly, etc. In 1975 we owned a Volkswagen Super Beetle, and I had Tracy unplug the seat belt ignition interlock mechanisms under each front seat. The Germans had tried to force people to wear their seatbelt if they wanted to start the car: Forcing Failed! I became obsessed with that air cooled car after disabling that device, wondering what else was being forced upon the people. That same year VW put a horrible, early and unready, version of a fuel injection system upon the roadway, and most of those cars never saw over 100,000 miles (about 160934.4 km). People are resistant to too much change, believing in what's 'tried and true,' because concession takes time. People will try to alter a new device or product to be like the old one they had." The Old Guy's couldn't pinpoint the man's heritage and decided he must be Bohemian, deciding to keep their wagers and bet on something else.

Jack could tell the man was attempting to make connotations (meanings beyond their definition); reading what the man said as "There is only one Tracy amongst the 1,000's of Tracy's in this world that I care about, because only that 1 is my daughter. Don't try to change her from who she is into something she isn't." After Jack Grasp grasped the existential meanings--though he'd never be dumb enough as to try to restrict Tracy's life or free will--he looked directly in Tracy's Fathers' eyes, bowed his head in agreement, and taking one meaningful breath said "In a free society all are free to judge. If you can't judge, you can't be free; but who are we to judge?" Jack stepped back, looked at everybody, then said "If I was to be picked up by a self-driving car, whether it be limo or taxi, and the car judged me unworthy to be its passenger, I'd say nothing; rhetorical skills (persuasive) are for humans, but using the scrap yard is a dandy answer for any and all machines with a classic Napoleon complex."

The self-driving car topic had now come to its head, folks wanting to get a ruling, with everyone giving their last rebuttal, making enough sound at once that people in the diner became aware of how good the acoustics in the building really were. They had pointed out that the Airline Industry has been flying on autopilot for years. Those that lived through the 60's and

70's remembered seeing pilots, firsthand during flights, using autopilot to socialize with the passengers and drink while flying. They'd theorized a self-driving car to be a Governmental Plan to make people more dependent upon them, knowing the persona (face that's shown) would likely be different than what's seen. The Old Guy's Group avoided "What If" questions, knowing that they'd only lead to more "what if's," though Armond seemed to be asking a lot of them. Arm asked, "What if I'm a mess, and I go sleep in a camper that my self-driving car's pulling, but while I'm sleeping the car hits a drunk animal--people give their pet dogs marijuana sometimes, you know." Mostly, the more realistic theories made sense, like using a few hundred of the cars as pizza delivery vehicles to test them in an open market; see what the feedback from the community was, earning a little trust with folks. The Old Guy at the right who had fallen asleep again reawakened, saying to the rest of the Old Guy's Group "Remember that guy, back in the War...military...let's see, he had something or another...Oh, and he mixed both AC and DC voltage, calling it BC (both current), attempting to run an unmanned Uncle Sam special model Cadillac into the enemy; his logic was based on FM and AM radio and the, almost plausible, ability to create AFM if they were inter-mixed. It was a beautiful theory, but awful. The car acted kind of like an electric lawn mower; utilizing an extension type cord to maintain electricity, but because it had the engine coolant--which can become flammable in the right circumstances, being made of ethylene glycol and propylene--in the engine and used a radiator there was no good outcome when the Cadillac ran over its own cord. They'd (the government) suspected the fiery outcome ensued from auto-ignition of the antifreeze; really a live wire shorted the car as it was being wired to a phone pole's transformer box, frying all the circuits by becoming a conductor; the positive and negative voltage destroying all the cars' transistors and capacitors, then an arcing fire making a horrible sound took it propelling forward into oblivion. The enemy was quite nettled (annoyed) as they'd watched the self-propelled machine, moving (minimally) towards them, while burning up . . . don't point your fireball at me, man! It was such a challenge to comprehend (for both sides, us and them) that it pushed the enemy back 50 feet and stopped them from attacking the rest of the day."

Anyone who was within an earshot's distance of hearing the AC/DC voltage story gasped, one fella even fainted: requiring medical attention. Jack lightheartedly laughed, then said "Add another reason to why a self-driving car is a potential self-driving explosive. Analytics show that the FBI should be concerned with a 'sidetracked' (stolen and reprogrammed) self-driving car; as it was supposed to just be making a pizza delivery but took a wrong turn into The Whitehouse with a bang-bang-boom mission instead. One may be used to hit-and-run a high ranking official, with the person in the driver's seat getting off using the excuse of 'I wasn't in control!' Heck, if the vehicle's mission is true, the driver can be shot dead speeding into a military base and the car can still get a BOOMING job done. Drug War Killings, Bank Robberies, Rape; all easy with the right vehicle as an excuse. In the slight chance one becomes a taxi, it must be programmed with a NY City cabbie driver's skill; built with a 'real' defensive driver attitude, as opposed to a Milton County, Georgia driving style; even with its 23% population rise over the last 100 years it isn't defensive cab driver quick. Recall with me that local fella with a real 'This is Sparta' situation-- a few years ago when he gotten so fed up with the Water Company he went into his backyard and drilled his own new water point; living less than a block from the river, his ability to hit and tap the water was easy. He re-plumbed his house, so as not to use any City water and he stopped paying his bill; so, the city shut off water service to his house . . . and all was well the first few months, but because he still flushed his toilets' wastewater out (city water and sewer service are the same company) through the normal sewer piping way, when he called for help with a back-up into his house from the sewer, the city declared it wasn't their problem." All the Old Guy's saw Jack's point and the loose discussion was over. The Old Guy's paid for their coffees and left the diner as a group.

CHAPTER 13

Jack started bussing tables (clearing away customer's used plates, etc.,) any dirty dishes and cleaning the counter surface, getting everything settled at the diner for it to be closed for the weekend. Suddenly, Arm burst in through the diner's front door and damn near ran across the place till he approached Jack, then he just kind of stood still as a statue, looking for the right words to say. Jack thought maybe Arm had finally learned the United States flag has 50 stars on her (not 48 anymore) while on his way over to the diner, and was running to see if Jack knew, getting hysterical about it. Once Arm stopped hyperventilating enough to speak, he explained to Jack "I just came from The Tavern. Tracy said she'll be late getting off tonight; an unexpected group of guys just came in, and she hopes to catch a later showing of whatever movie you're supposed to be seeing. Jack, listen . . . I just saw the group of fellas she's dealing with and they're no good.

One of the guys who's wearing an embroidered Coast Guard ball cap, who was already drunk when he came into The Tavern, groped Tracy's breast and laughed at her reaction--the swine thought he was being funny--in front of everyone! Tracy called the guys 'Annoying, Lecherous Pigs!' before I'd even gotten out of there to come get you. As I was leaving the guys were planning to grope Tracy and slurring 'Come on, Little Debbie, we want to see your pumpkin cookies.' Tracy's voice got the most precise I've ever heard, as if she was aiming a message to be delivered right to my ears--I was trained to listen for, watch and report any secret communists back in The War, relaying all information to watch commander--and she pleaded 'Stop it! Time for a reality check fella. My boyfriend will show you what and who's in charge, without disappointment!" Jack had been devising a plan since Arm first said 'groped' and because Arm's wartime messenger training had helped in some way, Jack said, "Thank you for your service!" and headed over to the phone. Armond recalled a burned-in memory fragment of an old-time Presidential Address, where the emphasis lies on how "Gossip is essential!"

Jack was staunch (strongly loyal) when it came to Tracy related things, so hearing the message Arm had relayed him, it's easy to see understand why Jack set aside his deportment (manners) while calling the Coast Guard Station; located right next to the local marina, across the street and over from The Steel Palace Diner. Arm listened while noting that Jack's call was transferred (several times, without hesitation) over to a slew of different ranking officials. Jack was saying things like "Moving is a big transition . . . diminution . . . pretext for the action . . . assumption (a taking) . . . process of reasoned inquiry." Arm couldn't help but arguably think he was witnessing a rare "history in the making" phone call; the kind that Hollywood loves turning into films.

CHAPTER 14

Meanwhile, over at The Tavern, Tracy had figured out that the group of fellas came from drinking over in the neighboring state, just across the bridge by the local marina. In that state, the guys had boughten a few "to go" beers from Some Bar, who then put the beers in a brown paper bag; allowing the fellas transport and to drink as they walked over the state line bridge. One of the guys had been hooting in The Tavern about how he'd been able to pee in the river that ran underneath the states' shared bridge way, while spreading his legs and keeping one foot on the riverbank of each state--after finding a narrow enough place in the river to pull a stunt as such. The man was laughing and telling Tracy "I was standing' there peeing, just a peeing! Hey, then a big old sturgeon fish swims under me while I'm still peeing, so I aimed right and peed on the fish. Peeing!" Tracy was disgusted, but the guy grabbed her and pulled her to him while saying "It was one of them spawning fish, so I pee more thinking' I want to spawn too. You want to spawn with me honey?" Tracy broke the guy's hold and started backing away from the group, shedding tear drops that she could no longer hold back: fearful. The brute started yelling gibberish to Tracy, saying "I can pee on you, because I feel good you look!" The drunken man had one of his friends pull downward Tracy's skirt while making spawning gestures at her. That's when Tracy heard her man, Jack Grasp, outside barking something to Rolland, with an echo of 7 or 8 men replying "American!" Tracy knew she was saved as every door of The Tavern opened simultaneously, and she saw that Jack had brought a certain type of select company with him.

Rolland came through the front door of The Tavern, bringing a Coast Guard's Ensign (junior officer) and an XO (executive officer) with him, while through the side hatch door Jack entered with a Coast Guard: Admiral, Master Chief and their Commandant himself. Arm stayed back inside the diner, in case one of the grope guys tried to sneak away through the hatchway and the diner--Arm would make sure that guy would never walk again. Instantly, upon seeing their superiors, the group of rowdy guys became ghost-like shades of white, one even took up the fetal position. Some clear, sharp and direct instructions were shouted to the guy in the fetal position by the Master Chief, while the XO stated he "owned" the guy who pulled Tracy's skirt. The guy who had had a Coast Guard embroidered ball cap swung around and marched out of The Tavern on the Ensign and Admiral's command. Tracy scurried over to Jack, letting out a sigh of relief. The Commandant said "Ms. Bedart, I am very sorry. The Coast Guard has failed you." Tracy found the apology touching, and said "Mr. Commandant, if there's one thing I've learned as a tavern hostess; it's that no one is 100% honest. The funny thing is we both have to deal with those guys you just wrangled up, only they wouldn't listen to me." The Commandant replied "The Coast Guard doesn't take Sexual harassment lightly. I can assure you that those guys will be dishonorably discharged and relocated." Tracy felt at ease and said, "Thank You." The Commandant left and Tracy rushed to hug Jack, knowing his concern for her was all that was on his mind. Rolland and Arm started to walk over to Jack and Tracy, wanting to discuss the whole event.

Rolland, though usually a conceded asshat, had to admit to himself that he was wrong for not having any security cameras or bouncers that may have helped stop such a menacing activity before becoming a problem; still he held to his poor inductive reasoning, hoping that Tracy wouldn't hold The Tavern liable in any way.

Rolland, sorry he'd put money before morals, apologized to Tracy, saying "Tracy, you're a significant part of this tavern's family, and I hope you don't think me callous that I was more concerned with the legacy of The Tavern and keeping it an old-timey establishment; free of having modern video cameras, wires, security alarms; which in the long run jeopardize your safety and the safety of others too." Tracy felt like that was a half-assed apology, even for Rolland's way of communicating, but then Rolland said "I've had my share of narrow escapes but come out without a scratch. How'd you do?" Tracy replied

"Brother, there are really some ragged mountains here!" Arm chimed into the conversation and told Rolland "Get real Roll! She's due for a promotion with all the bonuses and benefits you can muster up. Given what's happened, if Erle Stanley Gardner could've had Perry Mason defending this type of case in court, they'd have awarded it so she (Tracy) could own your bar and leave you homeless on Kensington Ave., PA. and you would still owe her beyond that!"

CHAPTER 15

Jack had seen and heard more than his heart could bear; when Tracy hurt, he hurt too, so to cheer Tracy (and himself) up he quickly he pulled a ring out from his pants' pocket--so much for the weekend's surprise--and slid it on Tracy's ring finger, fitting it perfectly and saying, "Glad you're ok babe!" Jack looked at Tracy, Arm and Rolland as he retrieved 4 tickets to the Cirque du Soleil show in Vegas from his shirts' breast pocket, handing one out to each of them just as the limo he'd ordered earlier parked outside the diner. Jack excitedly asked, "Vegas Everyone?!"

--THE END--

THE
SUMMONING

Voice of News Anchor: "A panel of jurors has reached a verdict, deciding on new regulations for Heaven. The jurors were told that 'Sense nothing can be known of it till after someone dies, it is to be regarded in a certain way.' Thus, their decision is like in a previous case, known only by first and last name of the person."

PART 1

Hanging on the wall, just beyond the foot of my bed, there were a few artifacts and some chains (about necklace diameter), as well as candle holders. The candles in the holders were all lit; individually burning with bright orange fire. On the far-right side of my room were two pictures, one hung above the other; and both pictures were attempting to depict Jesus. In both paintings the Jesus is dressed in red and blue robes, but his representations were different; being each was painted by a different artist, at different times, and using different types of paint-- one in oil, one in acrylic. In one painting the Jesus figure is sitting at a table, his eyes are closed, his head is cast downward and turned to the left (his right) and is holding his right hand up in a gesture of sorts; thumb, middle, and ring finger meeting to form an O shape; pinky finger standing up alone.

My buddy, Pat, who thinks like me about religion, decided to do a "summoning challenge" to prove which picture was of the real Jesus; so, we could find out which one was the imposter. The Book of Family Traditions has a chapter called "The Life-Giving Sword," stating that "In Buddhism, they speak of fundamental non-existence and fundamental existence. When people die, their existence is concealed. When people are born, the nonexistent is manifested. The reality is the same thing." We thought nothing of the ritual we were about to perform, but still took up a margin of safety.

Pat knew more about what the "summoning challenge" entailed than me, though I knew it would involve a state of trance . . . or some such thing. Pat lay down and got himself into a sleeping state--of sorts anyway--, though there was more to it that he never told me about. I can say that when the event was over, and I'd helped him sit up, I was very concerned for his mental well-being. He may never be right again!

PART 2

Here's what happened, as far as from my perspective. First off, while Pat was lying there, he told me to hold an empty, light blue colored, three ring binder. The binder was known as "Old 62," and was comprised of a thick, oddly textured material; making it perfect for holding sideways (like a clam), and loud when manipulated to open and close with a clap-like action. I was sitting on my bed, facing the candles, while holding the binder and making clapping sounds with "Old 62;" while challenging the lower painting of Jesus to "get" the other picture. It is worth noting that the painting I was commanding; giving orders to it like a dog, had Jesus depicted with individuals to his left and right sides, but their irreverent. Also, Pat was waking up the demons from within his trance . . . though they could've been anything--judging from my observed speculations.

Suddenly, the candles started burning angrily; flickering in highly unusual ways and popping like flint: Contact verification! I watched the candles in disbelief, being I'd burned hundreds of them before, though nothing like what happened should occur with a piece of wax and a wick. I wondered, was Pat putting me on? So, I really started laying into this "Lord," shouting and demanding "Show me some damn proof of yourself!" I'd began treating him like an attack dog, giving the command "Sic 'him!" and making him "get" himself from in the other artists painting. Like an out-of-control dictator, scolding and harshly threatening his people, I took on a similar demeanor--the demons that Pat was fighting, now had come to attack me too, but my mode was so far in that they, thankfully, didn't keep hold of me. I scolded Jesus, barking loudly "There can only be one God!" The power and anger overcame me as I scornfully cried out one final demand, growling "Come on!" at him.

The whole ordeal had become an exercise in religious bullshit. The flames started to die down, and then they flared back up, becoming extremely violent. Apparently, the "Higher Being" chose not to burn my house down; as the flames just woofed out, and the candles themselves were completely gone; burned into nonexistence. The artifacts near where the candles had been remained, as well as the chains being all draped along the now soot covered wall, where the fire had made its hotbed.

PART 3

Seldom will I admit being afraid, let alone of the kind that makes me get out of bed, but I did have some apprehensions (feeling wise) regarding the event while it was occurring. Pat and I had gotten through it alive, which was more like a constellation settlement. "It's finally over," was how Pat spoke of the occurrence.

-The End-

◆ ◆ ◆

1666

W oken from sleep in the dead of night

Screams and cries ripping through the quiet

I gasped and saw a raw, orange light

Jumped up, took my blanket to cover my face:

Fire has taken over this place.

With one last look, I held my breath.

Thought "God if you exist" and made way for the exit.

After I had made it out, it was apparent

No one else was around; their shouts could still

Be heard inside the flaming house.

As I tried to go back and help,

Thud, Thump; the roof just let-out.

Standing, shaking, my jaw dropped,

My family's cries had just been stopped--

Only crackling fire made sound now.

Day after dreadful day

I replay it in my mind.

The pile of ashes reminding me

Of a world gone by; a home, a wife & kids

And a prized garden...now just blowing soot around

This empty lot.

Yell out to the maker "Ashes to ashes, dust to dust!"

Why not just leave us?

This year of our lord

Sixteen Hundred Sixty-Six.

* Written after reading Anne Bradstreet's "The Burning of our House"

IMAGINING
GOMER PYLE

I magining an episode of Gomer Pyle, U.S.M.C.,
after they were filming in color (early episodes
were filmed in black & white), where the
enemy's driven Gomer and his companions deep
into the forest, where they're trapped. Pyle's down
(injured), his eyes are closed, he's breathing hard,
and his body is in an upright position (almost like
sitting); with his back resting against a dirt-wall
bunker. The scene has: Gomer Pyle, two nameless
soldiers, Sgt. Carter, and one high-ranking official;
all hunkered down to avoid enemy fire but are
themselves out of ammunition to counterattack--
or to shoot off, allowing them to fall back.

Pyle starts talking in his clueless and stupid way--as he always does--when Sergeant Carter interrupts him with a direct order: "Pyle, give me your bracelet!" The Sergeant, being Pyle's boot-camp commander, remembered Pyle had crafted a bracelet from 7.62mm (about 0.3 in) M-15 military rounds, back while in recruit training. The ammunition was all linked together; each round being as long as an adult's middle finger. Sgt. Carter had allowed Pyle to create and wear the bracelet "for luck," if Pyle would just SHUT UP.

The two nameless soldiers start asking Pyle "Whys Sgt. Carter want your bracelet?" Gomer Pyle, being a complete idiot, couldn't figure it out either, so told the two nameless soldiers "Gosh, I sure can't imagine." Gomer takes off the bracelet and hands it over to The Sergeant, but Sgt. Carter doesn't say anything upon receiving it; to which Gomer lets out (loudly) a ridiculous "Golly!" The Sergeant still doesn't say a thing; as the camera shows him unhooking the bracelet, then begins loading the belt (correct term for ammo of this fashion) of 7 or 8 brass-cased rounds into his M-15 rifle's breach. The camera starts slowly zooming in on the sergeant's face, which now has a big and toothy smile, reading as if to say, "That big lughead just gave us the answer out of here!"

-That's it-

TRADITIONS
OF POETRY

T one your inner Robert Frost

Corona 3 your Ernest Hemingway

Image yourself after Emily Dickinson

Form your own Walt Whitman

Theme just like William Carlos Williams

Inspire your "true" feelings, but

Language yourself after E. E. Cummings

The American traditions of poetry

Matrix an experience.

Light for the darkest times!

-End-

AFTERWORD

This book was created after condensing some of my writings into one publication. Hopefully, these works have given everyone inspiration and encouragement!

Sincerely,
Kenneth G. Kruschka

BOOKS BY THIS AUTHOR

The Caribou Cruise

A mischievous maritime adventure! Roger (the main character) takes his Ohio Machine Company friends and their wives on a two-week vacation on a ship he buys, known as Caribou, after listening to an Ohio radio broadcaster's advice on how it's the perfect time of year to explore the coastal waterways. Roger and his friends stay aboard a ship that none of them have great knowledge of. The story is told from Roger's perspective of things, in a daily "journal like" format, recording the drama that his group encounters in traveling to their ship, then nautically trying to overcome the East Coast's waters around Maine. As a group, they sail through events unknown to them. There's also a bonus story, called A.D. and B.C. in this book, which is the tale of a man (B.C.) who befriends a young boy (A.D.), and the series of daily events that lead the main character (B.C.) to reflect more on his ex-girlfriend, than that he might be the child's father. ISBN: 9798990136700 (eBook) ISBN: 9798990136700 (Paperback).

www.ingramcontent.com/pod-product-compliance
Lightning Source LLC
Chambersburg PA
CBHW071305210626
46818CB00015B/2963